THE IRON STIRRUP

At fifty, they said Fletcher Markley was too old to be sheriff, and they replaced him with a younger man named Buster Munzer. Riding away for what he thought was the last time, Fletcher stumbled upon a wounded man, and almost before he recovered from that, the outlaws struck Evanston again. Fletcher went after them in grim earnest, though the new sheriff reckoned that was interfering with the law. In the ensuing gunfight some men didn't come through alive.

THE IRON STIRRUP

THE IRON STIRRUP

by

CLAY ALLAN

MAGNA PRINT BOOKS
Long Preston, North Yorkshire,
England.

British Library Cataloguing in Publication Data

Allen, Clay
    The iron stirrup.—Large print ed
    Rn: Lauran Paine   I. Title
    813′.54(F)   PS3551.L392

    ISBN 0-86009-550-9

First Published in Great Britain by Robert Hale Ltd 1966

Copyright © 1966 by Robert Hale Ltd

Published in Large Print 1983 by arrangement with Robert Hale Ltd
London

Photoset in Great Britain by
Dermar Phototypesetting Co., Long Preston, North Yorkshire.

Printed and bound in Great Britain by
Redwood Burn Limited, Trowbridge.

CHAPTER 1

He was one of those big, heavy men with a Longhorn moustache who usually wore dark clothing and didn't walk into a room or a gathering, he loomed. Years back when Fletcher Markley had been a young man folks had said he was the only man in western New Mexico Territory who could go buffalo hunting without a rifle.

That had been in the days when buffalo hunters had to preserve their topknots from marauding Apaches, Comanches, Mexican renegades, and an assortment of white and cross-bred killers, murderers, bushwhackers, seen nowhere else but in early-day western New Mexico Territory.

Fletcher was a round-faced, clear-eyed, fifty-year-old hulk. He had a slight limp, so when he strolled the plankwalks of Evanston he rolled with the yaw and pitch of a big lumbering battleship. He was a quiet, orderly, peaceable man, in the afternoon of his life, who'd seen just about everything men could devise in his part of the world, and he knew human nature well enough so that if he'd been transported to Timbuktu it wouldn't have taken him more than a day or two to become thoroughly oriented.

He was quietly familiar with all the ways of treachery. *All* of them; and he didn't need to go to Timbuktu to know them either, for if the Apaches hadn't tried to practise them upon him, then the Comanches had. But if they hadn't, those historically treacherous people, the Mexicans, had. Or the half breeds; or the Texans and Missourians, or Arizonans, or the eternally smiling, black-eyed *Californios,* finest horsemen on earth bar none, and also masters at the genteel art of sophisticated treachery.

Fletcher Markley had survived them all. He could tick off the names of departed gunfighters, stiletto-wielders, bushwhackers, snipers, by the dozen, whom he had known. They were gone. Fletcher Markley was still around.

It might have seemed a little odd to strangers in Evanston that a man as renowned and big and formidable-appearing as Fletcher Markley, whose reputation had been established firmly thirty years before, should be the topic of local talk, misgivings, and cold, practical speculation. But that was exactly what was happening, and two-thirds of the town of Evanston were betting against their sheriff.

It wasn't that folks didn't appreciate all that Fletcher had done. Nor was it that they didn't like him, personally. He was head of his Masonic lodge in Evanston. He had once been mayor, and again he'd been a Town Councilman. He was formidable, yes, but he was also quiet and gentle, and, in days gone by, he'd also had that fierce-soft smile for people he met. Fletcher Markley was liked and respected and sought out for his opinions. He'd even adjudicated a couple of near range wars among the cattle interests, which were the mainstay of Evanston, without once drawing that big Colts .44 he wore. The one whose white ivory handle had turned a sort of creamy yellow with the passage of time.

It was just that Fletcher Markley was fifty years old.

Any twenty-year-old firebrand could down him now, folks opined. A man of fifty had no right enforcing the law with a gun. That was for *young* men, not men old enough to be grand-fathers—if they'd ever married, which Fletcher never had.

But the town was divided. The hard-bitten older men, merchants, saloon owners, liverymen, nearly every one of them as old or older, and also com-fortably well off now, said that at fifty a man was just in his prime. Mostly, those men had known Fletcher Mark-ley twenty or more years; had seen him stand up in more than one roadway shoot-out, and afterwards stand a round of drinks over at Doc Johnson's combination card room and restau-rant, untouched because he was as fast as greased lightning with a gun—with either hand.

In opposition were the younger men such as Frank Cowdrey, manager of the local stage office, or Jack Phipps the telegrapher, and also Buster

Munzer, who had been a cowboy for old Flint Manly out at Broken Bow Ranch until he'd opened up a livery and freighting business in town. It was freckle-faced, red-headed Buster who said the town should turn Fletcher out to pasture and import someone like Durango Fedder, the sheriff and town marshal over in Costa Mucha County.

Then had come the bold daylight robbery of old man Whitly's general store where nearly everyone with money for fifty and more miles in all directions kept their cash in the huge steel safe at the back of the store. The outlaws hadn't gotten a red cent because old man Whitly had hurled his fierce defiance in their faces. He'd flatly refused to open his safe, daring them to do their damndest. They'd done it: They shot John Whitly seven times, and killed him. They cleaned out the cash drawer, got something like three hundred dollars, and afterwards had raced for the northward mountains.

Fletcher Markley had gone after them alone. He'd neither asked for a posse, nor had one volunteered. He'd been on the trail two days and came back looking as wrung out as a tired fifty-year-old man with a game leg could look. To all the eager questions he just had one slow-drawled, quiet answer: 'Don't you folks fret none. I'll get 'em yet.'

Well. That had been ten days before, and Fletcher hadn't brought them in. As Buster told the boys up along the bar at the *Claybank Bar & Restaurant*, 'How in hell do you expect him to bring them in? He rides out, and comes back the same day, and them outlaws keep gettin' farther and farther away.'

Fletcher's old friend who happened to own the *Claybank Bar & Restaurant*,

Will Duran, blackly glared at Buster and fired right back at him.

' 'You expect Fletcher to *manufacture* prints, Buster? Professional outlaws don't leave tracks for babies to follow. He's been bringin' in their kind for thirty years, sitting upright in their saddles with elbows lashed behind 'em. Or tied belly down, salted down with lead. Why; let me tell you fellers about the time he brought in the Burdon brothers all by himself. That was in the summer of...'

Sometimes a man's best friends, with their best intentions, do him infinitely more harm just by extolling him out loud, than if they kept their mouths closed. That's what happened this time. Most of the younger cowboys and townsmen in the *Claybank Bar & Restaurant* that afternoon had never heard of the Burdon brothers. Their fathers had, but with one or two grey and grizzled exceptions, there wasn't a man among those bar flies who was that old. So what ensued was what would have ensued anywhere else; the cowboys got bored with Will Duran's highly coloured story and gradually drifted out of the saloon, making humorous allusions to Fletcher Markley—not Will Duran.

As old Arapaho Whitson would have said, 'It's the danged, cussed combination. Once the combination get to workin' aga'n a man, he's just plain whopped.' The 'Combination' was bad weather, bad talk, and bad luck. When he'd been above ground Arapaho used to point out with painstaking care just exactly how the 'Combination' worked. He'd had it worked out to perfection too, but then old Arapaho Whitson had been alive a long while—eighty-five years some folks said when he cashed in—and he'd been as wise as an owl for at least the last fifty of them.

But Arapaho Whitson was dead, and for all his strange and sometimes downright startling wisdom, he hadn't left much behind beyond abounding faith in Fletcher Markley, six hundred and forty acres of deeded foothill land, nine old horses, a sturdy log house and barn, and his daughter Cynthia— whom he'd always called Petl—his daughter from a union one fiercely cold blizzardly winter high in the trap-line-uplands, with a handsome half-breed Ute woman.

No one ever knew what became of the Ute woman. 'She died,' was all old Arapaho ever said on that topic. He'd raised Cynthia himself, taught her to read and write and 'cipher' although he'd had the devil's own time of it because he first had to teach himself those things. He also taught her to shoot and ride, to trap and read sign, and beware the 'Combination'.

Once, someone even recalled the

'Combination' when several local cowmen and townsmen were sitting in a poker game at the *Claybank*. The 'Combination', it was said that time, surely was working against Fletcher Markley. Maybe that was the whole trouble. Fletcher couldn't catch those cussed robbers because adversities were piling up against him.

'Or,' someone suggested, 'because he's just too damned old anymore to get the job done.' And another man said: 'You don't use an old ropin' horse after he gets stiff in the shoulders do you? 'Course not. You turn him out to stand in the sun the rest o' his life. Well; Fletcher's been a topnotch peace officer in his day. But...'

But on the fifteenth day after the robbery and murder something happened which very nearly clinched the ouster of Fletcher Markley. 'Pinky' Maddon was looking for some cattle he said had broken out of a fenced-in plot of land he had, back a mile in the foothills, when he spied this feller sittin' near a big oak tree near Ute Creek bathing his bare feet while his big old horse grazed around dragging the reins.

'Pinky' had ridden on down because he was curious, and there sat Fletcher Markley. He wasn't on an outlaw-trail at all, 'Pinky' averred, at the *Claybank Bar & Restaurant* that same night. No siree. Old Fletcher was sitting there smoking his pipe, staring into the water like a hypnotised man, bathing both his feet in the cool water!

No one asked Sheriff Markley about that. No one thought to ask him because it was just too good a story as 'Pinky' had told it. Of course, any other time although the other cattle-men and merchants might have listened to 'Pinky', they wouldn't have put a whole lot of faith in his words because he was a notorious liar. He'd been known to swear up and down to anything at all he thought he might benefit from, personally, like the time he sold a bunch of barren cows he'd culled out as calvy cows. Also, he was loud-mouthed, opinionated, pathetically ignorant, crude and so egotistical it was funny. Well; sometimes it was funny. Other times it wasn't funny at all. There was a joke among the cowmen that Maddon had political ambitions. What made it a joke was that although everyone else fully recognised the total improbability of Maddon ever fooling anyone but himself, Maddon thought he had everyone else fooled.

Still, as contemptible as 'Pinky' Maddon was, his story about Fletcher Markley stuck. It was repeated, embroidered, passed along outside the county, and eventually it even got back to Sheriff Markley himself.

He didn't let on that he knew. In

fact, he didn't let on that he was aware of all the other talk either, but he was. No man of Fletcher Markley's worth and good sense was ever blind to his critics or his detractors. But how did a man strike back at the tidal wave of snowballing adverse public opinion? He didn't. It was like the big old stag fighting for his life in a ring of slavering wolves. He could toss one, kick another, gore two or three more, but all he did by doing those things was gradually exhaust himself so the others eventually pulled him down.

Being lonely had a lot to do with it too. The men who'd come to New Mexico Territory about the same time Fletcher Markley had also arrived there—men like Arapaho Whitson— were gone now. Even the redskins were gone. There was no affinity left; nothing of the old ways and the olden times.

Being lonely bore these things in upon Sheriff Markley, without a doubt, but the iron in a man's soul which had kept him from bending through all the perils of a violent lifetime up to now, would not let him bow now either. Or at least it kept him straight and stalwart right up to the time the Town Council came to grips with the problem, wrestled with it back and forth for three days, then finally decided Sheriff Markley would have to be replaced by a younger, tougher man who was in tune with the times. Who might, in short, get that money back and catch those men who had murdered Old Man Whitly.

The problem arose, next, of who was to tell Markley he was through. No one would do it so they wrote him a letter, posted it, and the morning it was delivered to his jailhouse office every town councilman managed to have business out of town for that one day. They weren't ever very many heroes in the world anyway. Evanston didn't have a single one.

CHAPTER 2

For nine years Fletcher Markley had lived at the only roominghouse in Evanston. It was on a back road, fed well, and possessed a fine old broad, rotting wooden veranda where a man could loosen himself of a fine summer evening, smoke his pipe and watch the long shadows steal down from the northward hills, rocking gently back and forth with the sounds of the town around him, like the sounds of children.

The day Fletcher Markley received that letter of termination from the Town Council he didn't explode nor rush across to the fire-house and storm upstairs to the Council Room, letter in hand and fire in the eyes. He simply sat a spell, reading and re-reading the thing, then got up, took his hat, his pouch of tobacco, his coat and gun-belt, and walked out, went to the liverybarn with orders for his horse to be saddled, strolled around to the roominghouse to roll his blankets, and within a hour and a half after he'd received the letter he was on his way northward towards the golden-lighted foothills. Behind, the only indication that he'd ever, physically, been in Evanston at all, was his badge of office lying squarely in the centre of the desk at his jailhouse-office, and the manly scent in his room over the rooming-house, of his pipe.

Of course over twenty years' public service couldn't be wiped out that quickly, but the day he rode alone out of town with no one really understanding when folks saw him ride past, where or why he was going, was in every official sense, the last time Sheriff Markley would ride his old horse up through town and beyond, towards those soft-shadowed and heat-blurred northward hills and yonder mountains. If folks had known, they perhaps would have felt something; sadness, poignancy maybe, or just the fatalism which the near-sighted usually feel when they accept the passage of an era or a man.

He rode all the way to that pool on Ute Creek over on Broken Bow range a mile or two below old Arapaho Whitson's place, where 'Pinky' Maddon had spotted him that day, bathing stirrup-swollen feet. There, he did again as he'd done that other time; he set old Ned to dragging the reins while he browsed, removed his boots and socks, plunged both feet into the creek and sat in total solitude. This time, though, he didn't light up his pipe. At least not right away, he didn't.

It was hot. Few places on earth got as hot in mid-summer as Western New Mexico, and except that there were trees to get under and waterways like Ute Creek, the Evanston country could have vied with Arizona's Skull Valley or Texas's brush country, as an alternate hell.

He'd been there loafing for an hour, big and bear-like and grey with his years, before he filled his pipe, lit up and leaned his mighty back against the oak tree behind him, to study the shifting, high cloud patterns, an old horse turned out to pasture, but with one thing lacking—he had no pasture.

The way it usually was with ageing men, it was now with Fletcher Markley. The hurt was there all right, but it wasn't self-pity so much as it was abysmal loneliness. Maybe, if he'd had a family...but he'd never had one so that was that. All the earlier years were merged in his memory. There were high and low spots, some brighter than others, some darker too, but generally there was no distinct awareness of the passage of time; just a flowing tide of memories with no connotation of age or the passage of time connected with them at all. He was not, in his own mind, an old man. He was as strong, as fast, as durable as ever, except that his cussed feet swelled painfully inside his boots in hot weather now, and the print of newspapers kept getting smaller and smaller. Those were annoying but insignificant things.

His hearing was just as sharp too, only this time, he later assured himself, he was concentrating on something else, which was why he didn't hear anyone approaching until she stepped around into his vision, close to smiling.

'You were asleep,' she said.

He said of course he'd been asleep, otherwise he'd have heard her coming from back there to the east before she'd gotten within a half mile of him. She continued to smile at him. She hadn't come from the east, she'd come from the north, up where she lived in her log house. It was Cynthia Whitson, old Arapaho's daughter. They'd known each other since she'd been learning to walk and as the years had passed he'd often told her father she was the most thoroughly beautiful woman he'd ever seen.

And she still was.

At eighteen or nineteen, Cynthia Whitson was four inches over five feet in height. She weighed around a hundred and thirty pounds. Her skin was the colour of fresh-churned butter except in summertime, then it turned soft-gold. Her hair was as black as midnight but her eyes were that alluring and peculiar shade of grey a rangeman always associated with oak-smoke on a winter day. A kind of gunmetal colour.

She was large-breasted and flat-bellied; there wasn't an ounce of fat anywhere on her either. She was the kind of woman to make a man as old as Fletcher Markley tug rakishly at his Longhorn moustache, while at the same time being anxious for her safety. Once, a Broken Bow cowhand had written a song about Cynthia Whitson; it was said she and that curly-headed cowpuncher were in love. Then he rode to town one blast-furnace summer night four years back, took on a too-big load of whisky, and died in a gun-fight out there in the centre of the moonlighted road.

Then old Arapaho had also died—in his sleep, not in any kind of a fight—and for a year she never smiled. Except for that, though, it would have been hard to find any Indianness about her.

She laughed and was warm. If she had an enemy no one knew who it was, but down in Evanston there were some vinegary girls her own age, as flat up and down as pine planks, who fairly dissolved with green envy when she rode into town for supplies.

'They fired me, Cyn,' Fletcher Markley told her. 'They wrote me a letter saying the town had to have a younger peace officer. They didn't say any more'n that. Of course they didn't have to, really. I've felt it comin' since John Whitly was robbed and killed.' He puffed briefly to keep his pipe alive, then said, gazing up at her, 'What you doing down here, anyway?'

She came in closer, stepped into his shade and sank down near him. She was wearing a light brown split riding skirt and a white blouse with a white ribbon to match which held her great wealth of wavy black hair. Her boots were high-topped ones and her spurs were silver inlaid, after the custom of the Southwest.

'Fired you?' she said, incredulous. 'You've been the sheriff ever since I can remember. Why would they fire you?'

He looked into the creek, wiggled his toes, puffed a moment then said, 'Well, honey; when a man gets old it shows, you see. His jowls sort of sag, his hair either falls out or turns grey, and he thickens up a mite in the middle. Those are the external signs, you see, but inside, in his mind an' his muscles he's likely to be just as good as ever. Better even, because he's lived longer and is wiser. But folks can't see what's inside—only what's outside— and they figure an old peace officer just can't cut the mustard.'

'Buster Munzer,' she spat out. 'Frank Cowdrey and Jack Phipps. I know. I heard them talking one time at the general store.'

He shrugged. 'It's done. No sense in blaming folks. It's done and maybe before many more years are out I'll thank them for doing it.'

'Where...What will you do now?'

He smiled over at her. 'First off, I've got to shake off this feeling of being kicked in the stomach by a mule. After that—'

'Sheriff. You come home with me,' she said very swiftly, and sprang to her feet.

He looked up at her. There were mannerisms she had that reminded him strongly of her father. He supposed the other ways she had, the ones which were foreign to him, probably came from her mother, the half-blood Ute woman. 'That's right kind of you,' he slowly told her, 'but I don't think so, Cynthia. I'll just rest here a spell longer, then decide which way to ride.'

'Sheriff,' she said, bending down a little in her intentness. 'I want you to come home with me. I...I've got something I want to show you.'

He smiled a little, but his smile slipped sideways. He knew her very well. 'What is it?' he asked, removing his pipe.

'I thought of you often,' she murmured, seemingly having difficulty. 'Last week I almost rode down to Evanston to see you. Then I didn't. But now it's different. I want you to come back with me.'

He sighed, drew up his feet, vigorously wiggled them and started to pull on both socks and boots. Whatever it was, she was troubled about it. Maybe an old grave; there were lots of them around, left over from the Indian wars. Some left over from earlier fights and massacres, and even murders. He beat out his pipe in the creek, got heavily to his feet and went after old Ned without another glance or word.

When he rode around the tree, she was just hastening beyond sight around the low, full flank of a round hill where she'd evidently left her horse in shade. He rode on over and met her. She turned and loped straight north-ward into the low-hill-country where trees were more numerous, where Ute Creek came brawling down from the farther away highlands, until she struck a trail, old and dusty, over which she kept riding on without once looking back.

He wasn't in that much of a hurry; besides, he was inclined to favour old Ned. They'd been over a lot of trails together the past ten years; they'd very rarely ridden one that required speed instead of endurance. This one, he told the horse, was no damned exception, because it only led over to Arapaho's log cabin in the piny-clearing where Ute Creek swerved around a high-country bluff and ran almost from west to east.

He was perfectly correct. Ned took him into the clearing a good ten minutes after Cynthia had already reached there. Ned also took him across to the barn; he was a horse with a strong memory. Other times down the years he'd been fed and bedded in that log barn. The fact that the gamy-scented old man who used to be around this place was no longer here didn't change a thing. If the log barn with its loft of fragrant meadow-hay had disappeared, then of course that would've been a real tragedy.

Fletcher Markley stepped down; his feet still felt cool and hadn't started that infernal swelling yet. He led old Ned inside, off-saddled, stalled him and stood a moment or two in the blessed shade deeply breathing. There wasn't a log barn in the country with quite the same fragrance.

Cynthia came out under the wooden

awning over across the yard, so he stepped forward and started walking in that pitching, rolling way he had, straight on across to her. He was beginning to have mellow and indulgent thoughts. She was lonely too, and perhaps something had frightened her, living up here alone and all. He smiled and stepped up onto the porch —straight into the range of a cocked, black looking forty-five Colt pistol pointing at his belly from around the side of Arapaho Whitson's old oaken door.

Fletcher stopped dead still. His indulgent small smile faded. His rock-steady blue eyes slowly arose to seek the man behind that weapon. His Longhorn moustache bristled. 'Son,' he said evenly and a little thinly, 'don't you ever point a gun at me!'

The man was stripped to the waist with his left arm in a cloth sling. He had a bandage around and over his left shoulder, too. He was a young man, bronzed from many suns, lean and rippling with tight-packed muscle, but he looked drawn out, weak and tucked up. His hair was black and curly but his eyes were light blue. He was a good looking man, but hard. Hard as steel and with a fierce spirit that showed in the moving depths of his eyes.

Cynthia stood aside watching them both. Fletcher turned his head, indignant with her for leading him into this. 'What are you trying to do?' he demanded.

She said, 'It's not loaded. He thinks it is, but I took the bullets out the day I found him and brought him down here.'

Fletcher looked back. The young man was staring at that cocked gun in his fist. He raised his eyes to her. She smiled. 'I told you he was a friend,' she said. 'He's not the sheriff. I said he *used* to be the sheriff.' She stretched forth one hand. 'Give it to me.'

Fletcher had never been a person to wait for someone else to gain the initiative when a bared gun was involved. He went forward with surprising speed, struck that extended arm at the wrist, knocked the gun down and savagely kicked it out into the dusty yard. Then he raised a big hand and gave the whipcord young man a violent shove backwards into the cabin and followed him right on in. Jack Phipps and Frank Cowdrey and Buster Munzer back in town wouldn't have believed he could still move that fast, nor that efficiently, but that's how life was: Where the action was; where a man of action shown at his best, ordinarily was the spot where the sceptics and critics of this world— never were.

Cynthia came in, looking worried. 'Don't hit him,' she cried. 'He's hurt.

He's only been able to stand up the last two or three days. He didn't mean anything. I frightened him when I said you were coming. Please don't hit him.'

Fletcher wasn't going to hit him. He'd disarmed him. That was enough, unless of course the wounded man chose to fight, then that would be a bird of another feather. But there was no fight in him; he went shakily to a wall-bunk, eased down on the edge of it and looked from Cynthia Whitson to Fletcher Markley. His expression was that of a trapped animal.

Fletcher studied the stranger. He'd seen a hundred just like him; hard and tight-wound and dangerous. He wagged his head back and forth at Cynthia. He could have killed her; if he'd had all his strength back he probably would have to.

'Girl,' he sternly said, 'What got into you? This isn't some orphaned fawn or lost coyote pup or sick racoon. What ever possessed you? Why didn't you just come down to town and tell me about him? Why; he could've cut your throat in your sleep.'

CHAPTER 3

Cynthia's cabin had three rooms and a
lean-to kitchen. It was cool because of
the thick log walls and peaked roof.
Her father had, at great expense, put
in four genuine glass windows, one
facing each cardinal compass point.
He used to say, when asked about
those four windows, he'd arranged
them that way to catch all prevailing
breezes in summertime, which they
did, no one could deny who'd ever felt
the coolness, and yet Fletcher Markley
had been around in those earlier days
too; it was an ancient redskin custom
to worship in the four directions and to

have clear access to them.

The small breeze coming from around the northward bluff also came through the ajar front door. It was very pleasant. Fletcher stood in it feeling the sweat drying under his shirt. Much of his indignation passed as he said, 'What's his name, Cynthia?'

She answered right back. 'Howard Harrison.'

The wounded man's blue eyes sprang to her face. He seemed surprised she knew his name. Fletcher went to a chair, sank down and considered Howard Harrison. 'You said you found him about two weeks ago, Cynthia. That's about right. Did he have some money on him?'

She went to a handmade chifferobe, brought back a knotted bandana and handed it to Fletcher. Inside were a number of things. A gold watch with the initials H.H. inside, engraved on the back case, a little nickle-plated four-barrelled belly-gun, about .25 calibre and not lethal past a hundred feet, and three hundred dollars in paper money wrapped in a piece of waterproof cloth.

Fletcher counted the money then put it all back into the bandana and dug for his pipe. 'Mister Harrison,' he said, stoking up and fishing around for a match to light up with. 'Where is your friend? There were two of you. Where is he—and how did you get hurt?'

Harrison was gazing past Fletcher Markley's thick shoulder at Cynthia Whitson; it was a look of reproach. 'I guessed wrong,' he said to her, ignoring Fletcher. 'I wasn't as helpless as you thought, but it was like awakening into a new world when I opened my eyes and saw you bending over, changing the dressing on my shoulder. It was like being in a quiet corner of heaven. I thought you were the most thoroughly lovely woman I'd ever seen. That you were—'

'Mister Harrison,' broke in Fletcher, and cleared his throat. 'The wound— how did you get it? Your pardner try to kill you over John Whitly's three hundred dollars?'

Harrison gave Fletcher a blank look. For a moment he just stared, then he very gradually seemed to understand something, and finally he said, 'I had nothing to do with the Whitly killing. At least not directly.'

Fletcher puffed and nodded, un-ruffled. 'Then explain how you knew the dead man's name, and how you knew there'd been a murder and robbery, Mister Harrison.'

Instead of replying Howard Harrison looked around him. Finally he said, 'Cynthia; will you get my empty gun, please? It's out there in the yard.'

She went at once to obey and Fletcher's heavy brows dropped a notch. The empty weapon was harmless, but after a lifetime of sidestepping tricks, when Cynthia returned he held out his hand for the forty-five. She handed it to him. He kept gazing across the younger man. 'What does this prove, Mister Harrison; it's still empty.'

'Take your clasp-knife,' was the reply, 'and unscrew the grips. You'll find a piece of paper in there.'

Fletcher went to work slowly and methodically. Sure enough, there was a piece of coarse paper folded many times and presed very flat, wedged against the inside grips. The paper had evidently been wet thoroughly, then heavily weighted to press it so flat. Fletcher had some difficulty getting it unfolded and smoothed out. It was a wanted poster from the Territory of Montana, offering a five hundred dollar reward for a man named Carl Bragg, whose description followed. He was wanted for murder and robbery, was said to be extremely dangerous, and when last heard of by the Montana authorities had been in Utah, apparently heading southward.

Fletcher looked up. Cynthia was bending over his shoulder studying the poster. He said, 'Description doesn't fit this one, Cyn.' She agreed by shaking her head and straightening up.

'I've been following Bragg,' Harrison said. 'It's a personal matter. I located him once, in Vernal, Utah, then he disappeared again. But he'd picked up a pardner there, so the trail wasn't too hard to re-locate. It headed straight towards northern Arizona, then, at St George, Utah, on the Arizona line, Bragg and his pardner stopped a coach, killed a man, stole a thousand dollars, and headed easterly around the Canyon, then dropped down towards western New Mexico.'

Fletcher handed the poster to Cynthia who took it over by the window and re-read it. Fletcher wordlessly began putting Harrison's sixgun back together again. The only comment he made as he worked was a tart one. 'Mister Harrison; only a damned fool would risk plugging up the spring of his cocking-hammer by sticking that paper inside the handle of his gun. It was a fool thing to do.'

Harrison nodded. 'That's about how it turned out,' he admitted. 'I found them. I was coming down through a pass in the mountains behind this cabin. They were coming up the same pass, riding hard. I should've heard them I reckon, but I didn't. It's a pretty good trail up through there, ankle-deep in dust.'

'So,' murmured Fletcher, 'they saw you first and left you lying. You're lucky. But that doesn't explain the three hundred dollars. You see, Mister Harrison, that's the exact amount of money that was taken from John Whitly after he was murdered.'

'I had five hundred when I left Montana,' answered Harrison. 'That three hundred is all I have left. As a matter of fact; that three hundred dollars is every last cent I have in this world, right now.'

Fletcher finished with the gun, hefted it, turned it over and over, then tossed it over onto the wall-bunk beside Harrison. The story was believable, but then Fletcher Markley had only rarely in his long career in law enforcement, talked to outlaws whose stories hadn't been believable. What a seasoned lawman instinctively went on, although few ever would have admitted it, was intuition. They relied on that while making further investigation, and in the end intuition was either proven correct or incorrect.

Another thing Fletcher Markley knew too, was that intuition, despite all the mystic virtues ascribed to it, was proven by investigations to be incorrect just as often, perhaps even more often, than it was proven correct.

But regardless of his personal feelings, he was at the cross-roads now; the only course left to be explored was the same one he'd explored dozens and dozens of times before. He said, 'Mister Harrison; you're going to jail.'

Cynthia looked swiftly down at Fletcher from over by the window. Evidently she'd already made her judgement. It had been favourable to Howard Harrison. But she was not only entirely inexperienced in matters of this nature, but also she was a woman. Whatever else might be said of women, they were not notorious for being completely logical.

Harrison said, 'I've already lost too

much time. Bragg and Gibson could be almost back to Miles City by now. Their trail will be as cold as—'

'You're still going to jail,' murmured Fletcher Markley. 'That robbery and killing down in Evanston cost me my job as sheriff of this county. I'm going to square that one up if it's the last thing I ever do. You'll do for openers, Mister Harrison, because I don't have anything better. And there's one flaw in your story. Those killers ran onto you up the trail, shot you out of the saddle and kept right on going; they didn't even stop to search you they were in such a hurry.'

'That's right.'

'Then how is it you knew about Whitly's murder down in Evanston?'

Cynthia said, 'I told him, Sheriff. I heard it from some of the Broken Bow riders. They were back in the mountains trying to find the killers too.'

Fletcher had his answer, but he also

had another question. 'Where is his horse, Cynthia?'

'I turned it out with my animals, Sheriff.'

'Do you recollect the brand it was wearing?' Cynthia nodded, went over to a table, drew the brand on a piece of paper and handed it to Fletcher. He said, 'Good girl,' and pocketed the paper as he arose, winced slightly from a little stab of pain in his game right leg, and motioned for Howard Harrison to also rise. Harrison obeyed, but had to steady himself with an out-stretched hand.

He muttered, 'Get a little dizzy is all, when I stand up quick-like.'

Fletcher studied the younger man. He was tough and wiry, but badly shrunk in the gut and cheeks. He'd obviously had a bad time of it during his convalescence. Cynthia moved close to Fletcher saying, 'Don't make him ride all that way, Sheriff. He wouldn't make it. Look at him.'

'An' if I leave him,' responded Markley, 'he won't be here when I get back, either.'

Cynthia had the answer to that 'Stay with him. I'll go to town for you. I know what you're going to do. You're going to telegraph to Montana about the brand on his horse.'

Fletcher turned and gazed at her. That had been precisely what he'd had in mind. That, and lock Harrison up in the Evanston jailhouse. She was watching him, her smoky gaze dead-level and appealing, but without pleading.

'The answer would be back by tomorrow. If you have to take him down there by then, maybe he'll be stronger. Let me do this one thing, Sheriff.'

There were a lot of iron lawmen, but the hardest, most unrelenting of them had never had to face the golden

51

beauty of Fletcher Markley's old friend's daughter, and although Fletcher himself was a hard man in many respects, an uncompromising man, he was not without his soft spot nor his streak of gentle understanding. Besides, if she left them alone up here so far from everyone, he just might be able to make up his mind about this wounded stranger.

Finally, though, what decided him in her favour was a private consideration. The moment he walked into Jack Phipp's telegraph office down in Evanston and sent that wire, Phipps was going to ruch up to the *Claybank Bar & Restaurant* and tell all his barfly cronies up there that old Markley was trying to re-instate himself by digging up a suspect in the Whitly killing.

He told her to go ahead, and passed back the slip of paper with the brand on it. He also told her how to address the telegram to the U.S. Marshal up at Miles City. Then he went out with her and helped her saddle up. After that, he watered his horse, forked it more feed in the barn, and went down to the creek to wash. It was while he was down there sluicing off that Howard Harrison came walking up.

'It helps a little,' he told Markley, easing down upon a little bench old Arapaho had made beside the creek and beneath a giant old bull-pine. 'But even when you find I'm not one of them, it'll still take me another two weeks to pick up their trail again. Maybe even longer.'

Fletcher shook off the surplus water, gave his heavy moustache a fierce upward twist, then stood up drying off with a bandana, looking thoughtful and dead calm. 'Well,' he growled, 'if your story is true, Mister Harrison, I think we can figure some way to cut that lost time down a heap.

Usually, there's pretty fair co-operation between lawmen. In three or four weeks' time this Carl Bragg and his friend'll have struck again somewhere. The telegraph lines'll help me pick up their trail without makin' a lot of long and pointless rides all over hell's half acre looking for them.'

'The other one's name is Hank Gibson. I picked that up along the trail. He's a two-bit gunman, so they say. Bragg isn't though; he's as deadly as they come.'

Markley finished drying off. He stood there in pine-shade, massive and rock-like, gravely considering the younger man. He'd already brushed Bragg and Gibson out of his mind. Their kind was always dangerous. In fact, there were no other kinds of outlaw and renegades except dangerous ones. That didn't much worry Fletcher Markley. He said. 'Cynthia's a good nurse, it appears like, Mister

Harrison.'

The wounded man's hard, bright eyes softened towards Fletcher. But that was the only indication he gave that he'd even heard Markley's words. He stood up, waited a moment for his obvious dizziness to pass, then he said, 'Takes a little time for a man to get his bearings back,' and started towards the cabin.

He had his sixgun in its tied-down hip-holster. When he was a hundred feet away he came about, half smiling, and drew his gun. 'Sheriff,' he called softly, 'it's loaded this time.' He stood out there in the bright afternoon sunlight watching Fletcher Markley, who was motionless at creek-side, then he said, 'If you're a poker player, Sheriff, tell me: Did you ever try to draw against a royal flush?'

Fletcher stuffed his bandana into a hip pocket, lowered his head and started walking straight towards that loaded gun. 'I drew against one once,' he said evenly, still walking. 'And I got a limp to remind me of it.'

Harrison let him come right on up and halt, then he lowered the gun and said, 'I wanted to convince you of something. If I'd been one of the men who'd killed Whitly down in Evanston, I'd have killed you too, just now. That's the best kind of argument I know of, Sheriff. I didn't kill you—I didn't kill Whitly.' He holstered the forty-five, turned and started on over towards the cabin.

Fletcher stood out there a moment, watching, then he gave his head an annoyed little shake, blew out a big breath, and also went trudging towards the cabin. It was close to mid-afternoon; Cynthia wouldn't be back until long after sunset. He might as well wrestle up some supper for Harrison and himself while he waited. It was going to be a long wait. The reply to his telegram wouldn't arrive back in Evanston probably until the following afternoon.

CHAPTER 4

Fletcher was correct. Cynthia didn't reach the clearing until past ten o'clock. He and Howard Harrison had been sitting outside on the porch, talking a little, but generally just sitting in the moon-softened, warm evening settling their fried meat and fried spuds and black java. When Cynthia came across to the house after caring for her horse she looked at them both, then said, 'I wondered...' didn't finish stating whatever it was she'd wondered about, and passed on inside.

They heard her eating in there. Harrison said, 'You know, Sheriff; a man could hunt a long time and never find another spot like this one to settle in.'

'Her father thought so too,' murmured Fletcher, pointing across the creek towards the huge, half-hidden stone bluff where Ute Creek made its bend from west to east before it sashayed back west once more, then ran on down across Broken Bow range. 'Arapaho used to say when a man had mountains at his back, grassy open country in front, and water in between, he couldn't expect anything more on this earth.'

Harrison was smoking a brown-paper cigarette. 'He must've been an interesting feller, her paw.' He pointed towards the starlighted old log barn across the clearing. 'I looked that thing over; you ever notice how every post and stud and baulk is dowelled with oak pins?'

Fletcher smiled softly in the darkness of the porch. 'I've noticed,' he replied, and didn't bother to elaborate; to explain he'd helped build that infernal big log barn.

'And the glass windows,' said Harrison, then let whatever he was going to add, trail off into full silence when Cynthia came out to them wearing moccasins instead of her boots, sat down upon the low steps and looked up.

'Well,' said Fletcher, gently rocking, puffing on his pipe and waiting. 'How was Evanston?'

'I could've hit him,' she exclaimed.

Fletcher guessed whom she meant. 'Jack Phipps?'

She nodded, and starlight shimmered in her heavy mass of thick, wavy hair. 'He read the telegram and said you were just trying to pin John Whitly's killing on anyone at all.'

Fletcher nodded and puffed, his round, broad face a mask. 'But he sent the thing, didn't he?'

'Yes. He sent it. He said, if they answered it at all, the reply couldn't reach Evanston until tomorrow morning at the very soonest.'

Fletcher removed his pipe, peered into the bowl, tamped it lightly with a thick thumb-pad and leaned back again to consider the pleasant night. They'd answer; he was confident of that. But he hadn't expected an answer before the following afternoon. Maybe, in the past, when Jack had sent telegrams for Fletcher, he'd been indifferently tardy. One thing Fletcher distinctly recalled, and with no pleasure, was Jack Phipps's insolence at times; as though being the only telegrapher for a hundred miles in all directions made him something special. But Jack was young. Fletcher was *not* young, so he could be tolerant. At least older men were supposed to be intolerant, but there were plenty of times when it was right hard work.

He glanced from the corner of his eyes at Howard Harrison. The younger man had a faded old blue work-shirt on now, with his arm-sling tied around his neck on the outside. Harrison was sitting there in the quiet gloom watching Cynthia Whitson's profile. She had her head tilted, leaning against an old porch-support, watching the high-arched heavens. Fletcher said, 'Mister Harrison,' to draw the younger man's thoughts away from what they'd obviously been concentrating upon. Then he said, 'I got the impression earlier when we were talking, that you have some special debt you'd like to settle with this Carl Bragg. Mind explaining about that?'

'I mind,' Harrison said quietly. 'It has no bearing on any of this, Sheriff. It's a private matter.'

Fletcher wasn't irritated. He was a firm believer in every man's right to have secrets. He had a big hoard of them himself. But this was a little different; Harrison was under a cloud in the Evanston country. But Fletcher examined the dottle of his pipe, found all the tobacco turned to ashes, and leaned forward to knock the pipe empty upon a porch-post, thinking that, at least objectively, he had no more right to pry than any other common citizen. He was no longer a law officer.

He leaned back, pushed the pipe into a pocket and looked over where the creek was running past in an oily way under the stars and moon. For that matter, he could get up right now, go over and saddle up Ned and ride on up through the mountains without ever even looking back or thinking about Howard Harrison again. For the first time since he could remember, doing that—turning his back on a man under suspicion—wouldn't be dereliction of duty. He wasn't a lawman any more, and that was that.

Cynthia was gazing up into Harrison's face when she said, 'I have the bullet from your shoulder. Do you want it?'

That amused him. White teeth flashed in the sun-bronzed darkness of his face. 'Keep it,' he told her. 'Keep it to remember me by. And the fifty dollars I'll give you.'

She straightened up a little against the post. 'The bullet I'll take,' she told him. 'I don't want a cent of your money.'

'Why?' he asked quickly. 'You think I stole it, too?'

She stiffened towards him. Fletcher could see that from over where he sat. She jumped up, hastened past them both and entered the house, closing the door behind herself. Fletcher sighed, settled deeper in his chair and thought he wouldn't be their age again, and have to go through all the anguish which lay ahead of them, for a hundred thousand dollars.

Harrison looked over, puzzled. 'What did I say?' he inquired.

Fletcher didn't answer; all he said was, 'Son; you've got a lot to learn, a long way to go to learn it, and I wouldn't be in your boots for the best herd of horses in New Mexico Territory,' then Fletcher stood up, tested his game leg, looked over towards the barn, looked down and around at Howard Harrison, and gestured. 'Come on; you'n I'll sleep in the hay tonight. Nothing better to smell when you awaken in the morning than meadow hay curin'. Let's go.'

Howard Harrison arose, troubled and long-faced. Fletcher waited for the younger man to precede him down off the porch out into the ghostly yard where silence and tree-shadows lay on every hand. They had about two hundred feet to walk; perhaps only a hundred and fifty feet. On their right Ute Creek busily churned along. Fletcher remembered something old Arapaho had said one time. 'The best place to put a barn is where you don't never have to do n'more'n open a corral gate to water your stock.' and that had been how Arapaho had staked out his corrals. Ute Creek had been ditched so that a segment of it ran right on through. No horse of Arapaho's had ever gone thirsty because someone got too lazy in midsummer to hike over and water him.

They were at the doorless big maw of the barn when Fletcher saw Harrison pause, head cocked, body drawn straight up, alert. The older man stepped first into the darkness, then listened.

'Horses,' said Harrison in a low whisper. 'Ridden horses at that, not loose ones.'

Fletcher finally picked it up, a very faint, almost imperceptible sound which appeared to be coming on in from the westerly forest. He jerked his head at Harrison. 'Get back inside and keep out of sight,' he growled. 'They aren't using the regular trail. Anybody who comes slipping through the forest like this bunch either doesn't know the country, or isn't bent on any social call. Get back in there and keep quiet!'

They waited, listening, but either the barn cut off all sound, or else the riders had stopped back in the dark forest somewhere to the west.

Fletcher looked at Howard Harrison and got back an identical look of curiosity and wariness. 'Bragg and Gibson coming back?' he asked. The younger man shook his head.

'Why? That wouldn't make any sense.'

An idea struck Fletcher. He pondered it a moment in his careful way, then jerked his head and started walking back down through the pitch darkness of the barn towards the rear doorless opening. Back there, they had an excellent view of the yonder forest north and south, as well as dead-ahead. After Fletcher had made a long study out through there, well beyond the corrals out back, across the oily-running little ditched-off segment of Ute Creek, he turned and stepped close to Harrison, saying, 'You sure it wouldn't be some friend of yours, or maybe someone who's been shagging you like you've been shagging Bragg and Gibson?'

'I'm sure,' murmured Harrison. 'I don't know anyone down here outside of you and Cynthia. But even if I did, they wouldn't know I was at the Whitson place. Until you showed up no one knew Cynthia wasn't alone up here.'

'Yeah,' agreed Fletcher, lifting out

his ivory-stocked sixgun. 'That's the way I've got it figured. So this'll be someone *I* know. Not anyone you'll know. Now you keep that gun of yours in its holster unless I tell you to use it.'

Harrison sucked in a quick, short breath and pointed ahead into the watery moonlight yonder, with his good arm. Fletcher looked, made out the silhouettes of two men cat-footing it forward towards the rear of the barn, and nodded his head. 'Just settle back,' he whispered. 'I'll take care of this. Remember—don't use that gun!'

The vague man-shapes out there were difficult to make out for as long as they had dark forest at their backs, but once they got down near the corral stringers, out where the water ran through, they had cleared ground behind them and their figures were readily discernible. Fletcher put out a big arm to ease Harrison off to one side a little. Both of them faded silently back a few steps where they couldn't be made out at all in the darkness.

One of those approaching silhouettes over by the creek said something in an indistinguishable low mutter to his companion, then both of them turned to look over their shoulders. But as far as either Howard Harrison or Fletcher Markley could make out, there were no other men coming on from the rearward forest.

The strangers eased around, found a gate, glided through it, closed it with great care, then began heading with more confidence straight towards the rear opening of the barn. Clearly they were of the opinion that once they reached the darkness inside the log structure, they'd be safe. That was, of course, their most distressing mistake, but neither of them knew it until they paused, looking left and right just outside, then nudged one another and stepped inside.

Fletcher was standing with his heavy shoulders pressing hard against the rough logs of the back-wall, inside. He let those two men step in and stop, then he swung his pistol overhand at the same time he took two long forward strides. The nearest man collapsed with a wrenched-out sob. His pardner gasped, and sprang away, whipping around as he did so. He was looking into the tilted-up barrel of Fletcher's forty-five. He had a gun in his hand but it was at his side. He very wisely made no attempt to raise it.

'Get it!' Fletcher growled. Harrison moved around behind Markley, struck the gun from the other man's hand, flipped the stranger's coat open and ran exploring fingers up and down, seeking a hide-out weapon, which he didn't find.

'That's all,' said Harrison, 'unless he's got one in his boot.'

Fletcher moved up close, jammed his barrel into the stranger's soft gut and wrenched him half around towards the rear barn opening so he could catch a little moonlight across the prisoner's face. He looked, stepped back, said a harsh word and holstered his weapon. 'I thought so,' he snarled, and gave his captive a hard thump in the chest. 'All right, Phipps; who's the one I cold-cocked?'

'Buster, Sheriff that's Munzer. You've no right—'

'You pair of cubs,' growled Fletcher. 'Since when do you figure you're men enough to mix in with the wolves? I should've shot you both out there in that damned corral. I'd have been perfectly justified.'

'Sheriff; we were only trying to—'

'What,' growled Fletcher, mad and stiff and standing with both fists balled. 'What were you simpletons trying to do?'

'Well. It was the telegram I sent for Cynthia Whitson today, Sheriff. We got to talkin' about it, y'see, up at the *Claybank*, and we figured maybe you just might have really got on the trail of one of those men who'd killed Old Man Whitly, and we thought—'

Without any warning Fletcher Markley swung. His fist caught Jack Phipps across the mouth. Phipps fell, rolled groggily and got up onto all fours. Fletcher reached down, hauled him back to his feet with one hand and called him a fighting name. Then he shook him the way a terrier shakes a rat and gave him a savage shove backwards. Phipps fell over a harness pole, caught the thing and righted himself with a dazed effort.

'Who else is out there holding the horses?' Fletcher demanded, his voice knife-edged with wrath. 'Frank Cowdrey, I suppose.'

'Frank and "Pinky" Maddon,'

muttered Phipps, feeling his bleeding lips.

'Who told you to censor telegrams,' growled Fletcher, taking another menacing forward stride. 'Jack; for two-bits I'd take you over my knee right in the middle of the road back in town, the next time I see you. You an' Buster and Frank. Can't you find any better company than a cheat an' liar like Maddon?'

'Listen, Sheriff; since you left we don't have any lawman in town, so the others an' me, well, we thought—'

'What *with?*' snarled Markley, boosting Munzer to his feet, steadying him, then pushing him straight over at Phipps. 'Take this carrion and go on back to your horse. Get astride and don't even so much as look back until you get back to town. Now get out of here!'

CHAPTER 5

When it was all over and they were standing alone in the dark barn, Howard Harrison said quietly, 'You were a might rough with him, Sheriff.'

'Rough with him?' countered Markley. 'And stop calling me sheriff. That's the scum that took that title away from me. Rough on him? If I'd been sure, out there in the corral, I'd have shot a leg out from under him. He's been asking for that a long, long time, Mister Harrison.'

The younger man was quiet for a moment, then he wryly smiled. 'Make you a trade,' he murmured. 'I'll quit calling you sheriff when you quit calling me Mister Harrison.'

Fletcher was one of those men slow to wrath and slow to climb back down from it. He didn't answer. He instead stepped to the rear doorway looking balefully out towards the distant forest where Phipps had half carried, half dragged Buster Munzer. 'Damned whelps,' he growled and turned around looking at Howard Harrison. 'They won't be back. Yonder's the loft-ladder—Howard—let's get up there and bed down.'

It was hot in the loft, along with being fragrant. Fletcher opened the two loft doors, front and back, to permit some breeze to circulate. As he limped back to drop down in the hay he said, 'I pity Evanston if it takes their kind on in my place. And I also pity whichever one of them wants the job. There isn't a man among them.'

Harrison hadn't been thinking along that vein at all. He'd been considering a possibly natural result of Fletcher Markley's roughness. 'Suppose,' he said, 'when Cynthia rides back down there tomorrow, they do something to *her?*'

Fletcher reared up out of the hay, peering across at Harrison who was stretched out his full length, his good arm propped under his head, and growled his answer to that. 'I'll go for the answer to that telegram. She'll stay right here. If they want trouble I'll be right pleased to accommodate 'em!'

'No good,' murmured Harrison, turning his head. 'You've got to stay here and watch me. How do you know I won't ride away the minute you leave?'

'Well now I'll tell you how I know you won't ride away the minute I leave,' growled Fletcher, easing back down in the hay. 'Because, damn you,

I'm going to take you right along with me. And don't give me any of that stuff about not being able to stand the trip, either.'

'Fletcher; I never said that. Cynthia did. Anyway; I'm fit for the ride, and I'd sort of like to make it. You saved my bacon tonight, maybe tomorrow I can do as much for you, down in Evanston.'

'That's likely,' snorted Fletcher Markley, who heaved up onto his side and went off to sleep. He was perfectly satisfied Howard Harrison was not an outlaw. He had no idea what else the younger man might be, and didn't especially care either; what he'd learned a long time back was that if a man didn't scrutinise other men too hard, he could get along passably well in this life.

When he awoke, though, just for a moment he had a bad feeling. Howard wasn't there beside him in the hay. He swore, got up, gimpy-legged it over to the front loft window and peered out. Harrison was down there in the dawn light washing at the watering trough. He even combed his hair.

Fletcher went back, pulled on his boots, beat chaff and stalks off himself then laboriously climbed down into the barn proper. As he stepped outside Howard pointed and said, 'Someone's coming.'

This visitor, though, was riding up the regular trail seemingly making a painful point of being seen. Fletcher watched a moment, then went over and began washing at the same trough. 'It's Will Duran,' he exclaimed between vigorous dousings. 'An old friend of mine. He owns the Claybank *Bar & Restaurant* down in town.'

Cynthia came onto the porch and called over that breakfast was ready. Then she saw the horseman approaching and stood stiffly watching, until

Fletcher called back identifying him.

'Put another cup of water in the coffee,' he said, 'it's Will Duran from town.'

There was one obvious factor: for Duran to reach the Whitson place at this time of day, he'd had to have gotten up and started out long before daybreak. Cowboys and rangemen did that every morning from force of habit, but for a townsman like Will Duran to roll out before five in the morning was unusual. As Fletcher Markley mopped his face off after the cold-water shave, and began stowing his small effects, Duran walked his horse across the yard, unloaded at the trough and without a word of greeting, or more than spearing Harrison with one sulphurous look, Duran said, 'Fletcher, you darn fool; they're convinced now that this young feller here is someone you're tryin' to hide out on 'em. They say if he wasn't, then you wouldn't have been hidin' in the barn out here last night armed with rifles an' all, keeping a vigil.'

Fletcher curled his moustache expertly, considering Duran. 'You mean you rode all the way up here before daylight to warn me, Will?' he asked.

'Well, confound it, Fletcher, we've been friends a long while. I figured you deserved a better chance than this.'

Fletcher went on curling his moustache. He glanced once at Harrison, once over where Cynthia was still leaning upon that porch-upright, then he said quietly and soberly, 'Will; are you sayin' they're coming back here?'

Will inclined his head just once. 'A posse of 'em, Fletcher. They were in my place after they returned from here last night.' Duran gave his head a hearty shake. 'Boy; you sure popped Buster over the noggin. He had to get four stitches in the tear. Fletcher; John Whitly's folks came on from back in Nebraska, too. They took over the store and are runnin' it. She's a sister to old John. Well; she gave 'em ammunition free.'

Fletcher scowled. 'What does she know about any of this?'

'Nothing at all,' Duran conceded, 'but since when has that stopped a woman from havin' an opinion? Listen, Fletcher; they've appointed Buster Munzer sheriff to fill out your unexpired term. They even talked the Town Council into it. And it's not just Jack Phipps and Frank Cowdrey, either. It's that ridiculous "Pinky" Maddon and some of Flint Manly's Broken Bow cowboys who happened to be in town last night when they came back from up here. I'd say there's maybe ten or twelve in the posse.'

'When did they leave town?' asked Fletcher, reaching for his hat.

'They hadn't left when I pulled out, but some of 'em were gatherin' down at Buster's liverybarn. They'd be on their way by this time all right.' Will Duran paused, ran a slower second glance up and down Howard Harrison, then said, 'Fletcher; if you weren't protectin' this young buck, then just what in hell were you doin' in the barn last night armed with rifles an' keepin' a close watch all round?'

Markley murmured a curse and said, 'Will; we were fixing to climb to the loft and bed down. We weren't keepin' a watch and neither of us had a rifle. Howard here, heard them coming. We watched them come across the open ground out back of the barn—like genuine novices—and when Buster stepped in that door yonder I busted him over the head and threw down on Jack Phipps.'

'You did more'n that,' grumbled Duran. 'Phipps had a fat lip on him when he come into my saloon after they got back.'

'Well all right, Will: I hit him a few licks. I've been wanting to wipe that sneer off his face for a couple of years. Last night he presented me with the perfect excuse. I don't like him, Will. I never liked him.' Fletcher turned, dropped his hat on and hooked Duran's arm. 'Come on, Arapaho's girl's got breakfast ready.' He started across the yard. 'You too, Howard. By the way; this is Will Duran. Will; that's Howard Harrison. He was chasing the same men I was trying to find—old Whitly's killers. Only difference was—he found them and they shot him. If that makes a man a fugitive from the law, then I've sure been one a lot of times.'

As they entered the cabin Will smiled and said something pleasant to Cynthia. Like Fletcher Markley, Will had also been a long-time friend of old

Arapaho Whitson's. He'd also watched Arapaho's daughter grow into a very beautiful girl. When she asked him what the trouble was he tossed aside his hat, rubbed his palms at sight of the buckwheat cakes heaped upon a platter at the oilcloth-covered table, and merrily said, 'Nothin' for you to worry your head about, Cynthia. On a woman-cooked breakfast of real buckwheat cakes, I expect even an old cuss like me could go out there when those punks get here from town, and tree the bunch of 'em with nothin' more'n a willow switch.'

She got their coffee and although they asked why she didn't eat with them, all she'd say was that she hadn't meant to cause all this trouble; that all she'd done was find an injured man and brought him home so he wouldn't die up there in the mountains. Fletcher told her she'd done just right; the three of them finally got her to sit and at least sip coffee with them. She took a place beside Howard Harrison.

For a while after that the men were silent, each in his own way considering the approaching trouble. Finally Fletcher finished eating, arose and went to the dead fireplace to stand while he stoked his pipe. He was still standing over there smoking when they all heard the horses out back of the barn neigh and run up and down behind their confining poles. Harrison arose with the quick, supple movement of a young man. Will Duran was drinking his coffee. He went right on until he'd finished it. Then he arose. Will was a swarthy, heavy-set man not over five feet nine inches in height, but scarred and blunt and forceful. His eyes were nearly black. He turned them upon Fletcher as he belatedly arose and said, 'Well; they've seen my horse over by the barn by now.' He said it with a kind of quiet, grim resignation, as though it had been in his mind all along that if he'd been able to, he'd just as soon not have been involved in this mess. He went to the door, looked out, twisted and said, 'Eight of 'em, Fletcher. I missed count by a couple, more or less. They're at the barn lookin' around.'

Fletcher finally moved. He took his pipe and carefully leaned it atop the fireplace mantel, hitched at his shell-belt and rolled on across to the door, shouldered past Duran and stepped out to the very edge of the little over-hang-porch.

'You fellers,' he growled loudly enough to be heard by the bunched-up horsemen over at the barn, 'come on over here. If you got something to say, this is the place to say it. There's no one in that barn.'

Buster Munzer was wearing Fletcher's old badge on his shirtfront. He was also wearing his hat high atop his head because of the white bandage-wrapping underneath that hat. The men with him were mostly townsmen; Cowdrey, Phipps, Doc Johnson who owned a card-room and café back in town, and one or two others. "Pinky" Maddon was there, looking fiercely foolish, along with some Broken Bow rangeriders from Flint Manly's ranch.

Buster led the slow march across the yard. Buster led his horse along but the others rode on across, all of them narrowly studying the open door behind Fletcher Markley, the windows in the cabin's walls, and Markley himself. They clearly expected some kind of trouble.

Munzer halted, tapped his badge and looked up into Fletcher's tough-set face. 'I'm the law hereabouts now,' he said harshly. 'I could haul you in for knockin' me over the head last night, Fletcher.'

Markley's answer was blunt. 'Like

hell you could, Buster. Last night you and Jack were just a pair of common sneaks trespassing in Cynthia Whitson's barn. You didn't have that badge on when I cold-cocked you. Now what do you want here?'

'That outlaw you're hiding,' growled Munzer, his red face and neck getting splotchy with colour. He was uncomfortable. No matter how hard he and the others were trying to make Fletcher Markley appear small and old and unimportant, they couldn't bring it off. Too many years had passed during which the former lawman had awed them with his courage and his tough ability. Just talking a man into insignificance didn't work; they were just now finding that out.

'I'm not hiding any outlaw,' growled Fletcher, shooting a hard look around into all those watching faces. 'I ought to bust you over the head again just for suggesting that, Buster.'

'Then fetch that feller out here,' challenged Jack Phipps from his saddle. 'Go on, Fletcher; if he's no murderer why don't you bring him out here?'

Fletcher didn't reply. He didn't even turn his head. But behind him Howard Harrison glided forward out of the cabin, and right behind Harrison came Will Duran. The possemen gazed with strong curiosity at Harrison. Then they looked accusingly at Will. Phipps said, ' 'Thought you could out-ride us didn't you, Will?'

Duran curled his dark lip and glared his scorn. 'I *did* out-ride you,' he sneered. 'But hell; for a bunch like you I could've done it on foot. Who do you think you are?'

'We been deputised by Sheriff Munzer,' piped up 'Pinky' Maddon, affecting that fierce-foolish look of his, ready to fight Will Duran, but only because he *would* fight, not because he was capable of the deep mental conviction that anything worth fighting for had been violated.

'Hell,' spat out Duran, looking them over one by one. 'Buster's no more qualified to be sheriff than I am. Sheriffs are *elected*, Maddon, they aren't just appointed. And it'd take more than an appointment to make a man a worthwhile peace officer anyway.'

'Never mind all this talk,' exclaimed Jack Cowdrey, pointing a finger at Harrison. 'We want that feller.'

'On what grounds?' Fletcher asked. 'If you don't have something pretty valid, and you lock him up, boys, then it turns out he's innocent of any crime, let me tell you something about the law I don't think you know: He can sue the county and every blessed one of you for false arrest—and win in the courts —and get judgement against each of you that'd strip you down to your socks and underwear.'

One of the Broken Bow cowboys rubbed his jaw and looked at another Broken Boy cowboy. 'Lem,' he said to his companion, 'I'm beginnin' to figure we got talked into somethin' last night. Let's get on out o' here.' Lem nodded, turned his horse and started riding. The other rangemen also rode back the way they'd come. The townsmen squirmed in their saddles. Jack Cowdrey, with vested interests in town, said, 'Fletcher; 'you give your word this feller isn't one of them as killed John Whitly?'

Fletcher shook his head. 'Frank; I wouldn't give you boys my word about anything. I don't have to. It's *you* that's got to prove something; you're the ones who are making the charges. All I'll tell you is that I'll testify in court if Howard Harrison brings suit against the lot of you, that the lot of you came out here, trespassed, and took this young man away by force, without showing a warrant and without proving your charges. And that, Jack, is the grounds for a suit for damages on the grounds of false arrest.'

Cowdrey shot a worried look over at Jack Phipps. The telegrapher looked down where Buster Munzer was standing, gazing straight up at Fletcher Markley. Cowdrey said, 'Buster; maybe we were a mite hasty.'

Buster's answer was sullen. 'He hit me over the head.'

Fletcher grinned. '*I* hit you over the head, Buster. If that's what's eating you, why, arrest me.'

'Aw hell,' growled Will Duran, looking disgusted, then he turned and brushed past Harrison to go back inside.

For a moment the possemen looked after Duran, then they looked down at Buster. Doc Johnson, who was older than the others, lifted his rein-hand as though to turn and ride off. Up to now he hadn't said a word, he'd just listened and watched. But now he spoke up in a slow, Texas-drawl. 'Buster; come on. I never agreed to settle any scores just because you got knocked down last night. The way this thing's goin', I don't want to be part of it, either.'

Doc started riding away. The others began following him. Munzer then got astride and also departed.

CHAPTER 6

Will Duran summed it up when the four of them strolled over to care for their horses at the barn. 'That was right childish. From start to finish, it was silly. The kind of thing kids do, not grown, mature men.'

Fletcher winked at Cynthia. He was feeling much better. 'Folks,' he opined, 'can grow up; they always do—but mostly only in the body. If there was a way to measure the brain-power of people in this world, darned if I don't think it'd be real surprising how many brains quit developing after about age ten.'

Howard Harrison paused at the water trough to scoop up a handful of clear water and trickle over the shoulder-bandage he was wearing. Will and Fletcher kept on striding along. Cynthia paused back there, looking puzzled. Howard said, 'The darn hot weather in this country dries out my wound. The cloth sticks to it. I try to keep the thing moist. It doesn't stick and it feels cooler.'

Fletcher paused, looked back, shrugged and walked on with Duran. At the barn, Will took his saddled horse inside to let it stand a while in the coolness. He loosened the cincha, slipped off the bridle and tied the critter in a tie-stall where the manger was half full of meadow hay, mostly Timothy Red Top and wonderfully fragrant. Will then pushed back his hat, started making a smoke, and said, 'Fletcher; why don't you come back? Listen to me; when that bunch of pups gets back and the word spreads what tomfools they made of themselves out here, folks are going to have a lot of second thoughts. They'll make the Town Council hire you back on again.'

Fletcher didn't even answer that appeal. He could see Cynthia and Howard Harrison talking together out there in the burnished sunshine by the trough. He said, 'Reckon I'll ride down to town with you, Will, and bring young Harrison along. I want to get the reply to a telegram I had sent yesterday.'

Duran lit up, peered sceptically out of narrowed eyes, and exhaled a long cloud of bluish smoke. 'All right; I won't say anything more about you comin' back, Fletcher. I've had my say on that. I reckon it's not really any of my affair anyway. But if you take Harrison and ride into town, Phipps'll likely try to give you another hard time. He and Buster and Frank

Cowdrey are pretty sore at you. You made them look ridiculous even in their own eyes, out here.'

Fletcher shrugged, groped in his pockets for his pipe, remembered he'd left it on the mantel over at the house and quit rummaging for it. 'You ready to start back?' he asked.

Duran nodded. He was ready. He still had that other matter on his mind, obviously, though, for he said, 'Be nice to have you in the roominghouse again.'

Fletcher fixed Duran with a stare. 'Will; I reckon when a man gets our age he turns a little vindictive. Right now I wouldn't hire out to the Town Council again for five times the pay I got before. They appointed Buster in my place. Let them live with that for a while. Well; let's get saddled up and heading for town. I'd like to get the telegram and return ahead of night-fall.'

Duran muttered, 'Sure,' and turned to watch Fletcher stride to the door and call for Howard Harrison to come catch his horse. Howard came at once. So did Cynthia. She stopped in front of Fletcher looking inquiringly up into his face. As young Harrison moved past with a bridle in hand, bound for the corrals, she said, 'It's awfully hot this morning, and his wound troubles him when it dries out. Why can't he...?'

Fletcher was shaking his head at her without saying a word. She looked over where Will was watching them. Duran turned discreetly and went after his mount. This was no affair of his and he clearly had no wish to be drawn into it.

Cynthia stood a moment after Fletcher had turned to go after his stalled saddle animal, then she too began moving, swiftly and expertly. She took down a bridle and went after a horse. Fletcher, peering across the back of his horse, was about to say something when Will Duran turned and shook his head, lifted his shoulders, dropped them resignedly, and rolled his eyes, saying in a mute way that it really didn't make a whole lot of difference if she went along, and also that it was easier to appease women than to argue endlessly with them. Evidently, for a bachelor, Will Duran wasn't entirely inexperienced in this field. Fletcher went back to work.

When they were all rigged out and ready, Fletcher went to the house, got his pipe, beat it empty on one hand while he crossed back to the barn where the others waited, then the four of them rode out of the yard, down through the final fringe of forest and out upon the shimmering, sunblasted range beyond, where heat rolled up and over them in ceaseless waves.

Cynthia had a canteen slung to the

swells of her saddle. No one commented about this although the ride wasn't so distant, nor the waterways so remote, that a canteen was necessary. An hour and a half later, Will Duran and Fletcher Markley saw why she'd brought that thing along. She and Howard Harrison were riding together behind the older man, talking a little now and then, when Cynthia held out the canteen. 'Moisten the bandage,' she said, and Howard did so.

Duran cocked a shrewd black eye at Fletcher, and gravely winked. Fletcher chuckled.

They came in sight of the pool where Fletcher had been loafing, soaking his feet, the day before, and kept right on riding. They saw some Broken Bow riders hazing a herd of saddle stock from east to west, and moments later were passing through the roiled dust that drive had scuffed to life. There wasn't a breath of air; it was hot and still and acrid-scented all around them. When they finally had Evanston in sight, far ahead and hull down upon the shifting horizon, Duran shook his head and morosely said, 'You know, Fletcher, there are two things in this life I never liked: Trouble and stud-horses, and I'll be darned if Fate doesn't seem to get some kind of delight out of saddlin' me with one or the other every time I turn around.'

'Stud-horses...?' Fletcher murmured, looking at his old friend.

'Yeah, stud-horses. Miss Whitly's got one. Old John's sister who came on from Nebraska to take over the store. I was helpin' her get down from her rig. I never noticed the cussed animal between the shafts was a stud-horse. He turned his head and give me a right painful nip as I was helpin' her down. It hurt, the baggy-eyed old reprobate. If she hadn't been standing right there

I'd have taken me an oak spoke and worked him over. But all I could do was grit my teeth and grin while she told me how sorry he was. It still hurts.'

Fletcher's eyes kindled with genuine mirth. 'Where did he bite you, Will?'

Duran turned a sardonic squint upon Markley, snorted and didn't reply to that. All he said was, 'Bit by a stud-horse yesterday, and up to my ears in trouble today. It's not very often a man gets *both* his pet aversions down on him within twenty-four hours is it?'

Fletcher, his eyes twinkling, soberly said, 'Will; it's the Combination. You recollect how Arapaho used to—?'

'I remember,' growled the saloon-owner. 'I remember darn well. And maybe he's right, too.' Duran rode along in silence for a while, studying the dust rising above the onward town. Then he said, 'Well; I reckon I can avoid that cussed old stallion easy enough from here on out. But what about the trouble?'

'There won't be any,' said Fletcher, also considering the town up ahead. 'They'll fume and stamp around, but they're not foolish enough to push for real trouble, Will. Not that bunch. Besides; they'd need more'n just Buster getting a crack over the head to fire the town up against me.'

Duran rode in silence again, his expression dark and resentful. It seemed almost as though he didn't like the town. Finally he said, 'I don't understand people, Fletcher. You've been keepin' order around the Evanston country since before most of 'em were old enough to vote. If it hadn't been for you a dozen times I could name, they'd have had gunmen takin' over. And yet they'd turn on you. I'll tell you somethin' for a fact: Some of my best friends are horses an' dogs!'

They came to the outskirts, passed down where there was a little shade, and because this hottest time of day nearly everyone was indoors, didn't see a soul until they were half way along towards Duran's saloon, then a pair of drooping Broken Bow cowboys came shuffling out of the stage office carrying a ranch mail-pouch. The cowboys stopped and stared. They had been in that posse earlier, up at the Whitson place. Fletcher looked straight at them and rode on. Behind him, Howard Harrison eased his right hand down and let it rest lightly upon his right thigh, not very far from his holstered sixgun.

But there was no fight in the Broken Bow men; they simply stood there staring.

In front of old John Whitly's store Fletcher caught sight of several people inside, lined up along the counter. Beyond, where the telegrapher's sign was, he veered in and stepped down. Will did the same. So did Howard Harrison and Cynthia Whitson. They stood together for a moment gazing around. Except for those two cowboys, standing up there in front of the stage office like they'd taken root and were unable to move, no one was abroad. 'Quiet enough,' observed Fletcher, looping his reins and turning to pass inside. Will Duran wrinkled his nose as though he were catching a scent of some kind. As Cynthia and Howard stepped past he said, 'Yeah; *too* quiet, even for this time o' day,' then trooped on inside with the others.

Jack Phipps was listening to his telegraph key and writing slowly upon a yellow pad of paper when the four newcomers lined up along his scarred pine counter. He didn't look up and they didn't interrupt. Whatever was coming through that little box where his receiver was located, had Jack

Phipps entirely engrossed. Fletcher fished out his pipe, filled it, struck a match and lit up. Will Duran, leaning at his side, twisted to look out into the shimmering roadway. Will had a puzzled frown across his face. He still acted like a dog catching an unusual odour.

Then Phipps closed his key, raised his head, and his eyes sprang wide open. He seemed frozen in his chair. Fletcher removed his pipe, beginning to scowl, and said, 'What's the matter with you?' to Phipps. 'You act like a man who just saw a ghost.'

Phipps glanced at the scribbling on his yellow tablet and up again. He got stiffly to his feet craning for a look outside into the yonder roadway. Will Duran, facing forward now, turned again to face in the same direction. He said very softly, almost sighing as he spoke, 'Well, Fletcher; we sure guessed wrong this time. Look yonder.'

They all turned, Cynthia, Harrison, and Fletcher. Converging upon the telegraph office, guns out and ready, were at least a dozen men including those two Broken Bow cowboys who'd turned to stone up in front of the stage office when Fletcher had led his little party into town. Out front was Frank Cowdrey looking pale and agitated, but also looking very resolute.

Fletcher swung back towards Phipps and found himself staring into the two bores of a shotgun. Phipps said, 'Now, Fletcher; don't you try anything.' Phipps was as grey as slate. 'Harrison —Will—Miss Whitson; you folks stand real easy now. If you act up you'll get cut to pieces.'

'What in the hell do you think you're doing?' growled Fletcher, nonplussed and indignant, both. Several men stamping inside from across the board plankwalk brought Fletcher back, facing in the other direction again. Frank Cowdrey pointed his sixgun straight at Howard Harrison, but the way he was standing in the doorway, with a dozen other armed, intent men crowding up behind him, he could also watch Fletcher.

'Harrison,' Frank said, his voice high and uncertain. 'You're under arrest.'

No one said anything for a moment after that. Fletcher was gazing at the men outside upon the plankwalk. He seemed to hesitate; seemed to believe this wasn't a bad joke or a poor attempt by some humiliated men to get even. In a quiet way he said, 'Frank; what's goin' on here?'

Cowdrey stepped back and muttered at several of the men outside to go over and disarm Harrison. They moved in at once, grim and determined. Harrison offered no resistance. Then one of the men moved with a black look upon Fletcher Markley, obviously intent upon taking his weapon also. Fletcher drew up off the counter. 'Don't you try it,' he warned, and the cowboy stopped in his tracks, still glaring, but a lot less resolute all of a sudden.

Cowdrey said, 'Jack; give Fletcher that answer to his telegram. Then let him see them other two.'

Phipps put down his scattergun with enormous relief, picked up several yellow pieces of paper, tore off the fresh one he'd just been writing on when Fletcher and the others walked in, stepped across and spread them out on his countertop.

Fletcher turned and bent down to read. So did Will Duran. Cynthia and Howard Harrison stood too far off, watching the armed men who were in turn also closely watching them.

For five full minutes it was so quiet in the telegraph office the wall-clock sounded unusually loud as it rhythmically and indifferently ticked off the seconds and minutes. Fletcher heaved a mighty sigh when he finished reading, turned and looked straight at Howard Harrison.

'Well,' he said in a dull, tired voice, 'Howard; I reckon you don't have to explain why you were after those two who shot John Whitly at all. The whole thing's there behind me on the counter. You're wanted in Montana in connection with the same murder Bragg and Gibson are wanted for.' He gazed at Will Duran, at Frank Cowdrey, and reached up to re-settle the hat atop his head. 'I made a mistake,' he said. 'All right; what do you want to do about it?'

Cowdrey gestured towards Harrison and spoke to the same men who'd disarmed him. 'Take him over an' lock him up,' he said, then lowered his weapon as the hard-faced possemen grabbed Harrison and started roughly towards the door with him. 'For you, Fletcher—nothin'. You did a foolish thing, but this town remembers you when you weren't fuzzy-minded. Just get on your horse and clear out of Evanston. Go on; take the girl with you.'

CHAPTER 7

Fletcher didn't argue He scooped up
those telegrams, shoved them into a
pocket and shuffled back outside into
the fierce yellow sunshine. Cynthia
went with him; so did Duran, who
shouldered the few idlers aside with
unnecessary roughness, went out to the
horses with Cynthia and Fletcher, then
said, 'Fletcher; that's all it was—a
mistake. They can't run you out of
town like this. You can't let them do
this to you.'

From the edge of the plankwalk
Frank Cowdrey said, 'Will; go on up
to your saloon. Stop meddling in

things that don't concern you.'

Duran turned, black-eyed and angry. 'You overgrown jack-snipe,' he growled, bristling and ready to fight, 'Since when do you give orders in this town?'

'Since Sheriff Munzer rode out a while back, makin' a sashay westerly over to Manly's place to borrow a handful of Broken Bow riders to use as a posse when he went back up there to Whitson's to arrest Harrison. He appointed me his deputy until he got back.'

Fletcher untied. Cynthia was already astride her horse. Fletcher paused and turned, gazing back at Frank Cowdrey. 'Buster is looking for Harrison?' he asked.

Cowdrey hooked both thumbs in his shell-belt and nodded, looking a lot more confident now than he'd looked ten minutes earlier. 'Yeah. We got the first telegram from the U.S. Marshal in Miles City, Montana, right early this morning, Fletcher. It was in reply to the one Cynthia sent yesterday. Phipps was waitin' for it. He fetched it right up to the saloon where we all saw it. The brand on Harrison's horse is a Montana mark all right. You've got the telegram, Fletcher, read it again on the way out of town. The brand was also on the horse, answering the same description as Harrison's horse, of a bank messenger killed by three outlaws —one of which was identified from a distance by a feller who rode with him as Howard Harrison. And Harrison had the guts to ride into Evanston on that dead man's horse.' Cowdrey kept looking down his nose at Fletcher. 'And you had the guts to try'n make out he could sue us for false arrest. Fletcher; for my part I wasn't real pleased about the talk to oust you. But after what's happened today, I reckon maybe we put it off too long.'

Cowdrey gestured. 'Mount up and ride on out.'

Will stepped away as Fletcher stepped up over his saddle and reined back before turning northward up the roadway. He and Cowdrey, and about eight other men gathered behind Cowdrey, traded long, hard looks. Will Duran remained out where he was beside the hitchrack watching Fletcher Markley ride up the road. He muttered, 'I don't believe it. I just don't believe Fletcher made no such a mistake.'

One of the men with Cowdrey laughed. 'Will,' he called. 'Lucky thing all you got is the *Claybank,* or folks'd be runnin' you out o' Evanston too, for being too old.'

Frank Cowdrey turned on that man and silenced him with a rough command. Then he and the others turned to watch the girl and the former sheriff boot their mounts over into a slow lope, clear the north end of Evanston, and keep right on going up through the heat-hazed, smoky day, back towards the far-away foothills.

Will Duran took his horse by the reins, led it dejectedly down to Cowdrey's liverybarn and tossed the reins to a hostler. Then he removed his hat, mopped sweat, and stood for a while peering far out northward, straight on up through town where he could distantly and very vaguely make out those two riders.

For a while he stood looking. Up the road Frank Cowdrey was joined out front of Duran's saloon by Jack Phipps and another man or two. They turned, finally, talking loudly among themselves, and went trooping on into the *Claybank Bar & Restaurant*. Will had a good bartender running things in there so he didn't waste a second thought on those men.

What interested him all of a sudden

was that it looked as though Fletcher
had split off from Cynthia and was
riding westerly out over the heat-
blurred range. Will removed his hat,
mopped off sweat, replaced the hat
and walked on down through
Cowdrey's liverybarn and out back.
From there, he crossed through an
empty plot where a slag heap of refuse
had been hurled for a long while,
making a mound nearly as tall as a
man, marched out between two un-
painted residences, narrowly avoided
being bitten by a dog not much larger
than a cat, and emerged out upon the
westward edge of town.

He didn't see a soul out there, now.
Neither Fletcher Markley nor a Broken
Bow rider, nor even a critter. He
moved back into some shade near a
hen-roost, rubbed his eyes and looked
again. That time he saw him; he was
just coming up out of an arroyo far
out, still bearing southerly down the

far side of town. Duran knitted his brows, trying to puzzle out what Fletcher was up to. Finally though, he sighed, swore with great feeling under his breath, and went stamping back to the liverybarn where he bawled for another horse, not his own, to be rigged out for him, and after that had been done, he flipped the day-man a half dollar, dragged himself into the saddle and said, 'A man's got to be fried in the brains to ride out in weather like this.' The hostler grinned and agreed, then tested the merit of the half dollar Will had given him by using big white, powerful teeth to see if he could dent it. He couldn't; the coin wasn't counterfeit.

Duran poked his horse in and out, back and forth, until he'd left the last shack and shed behind, then he sat still a moment peering from beneath the tugged-low brim of his hat for sign of Fletcher Markley once more, and when he finally caught the pale, far-off movement he went riding straight towards it.

Duran kept watching with powerful concentration, for it was blazing hot out there, the distances were mirage-like; they'd hurtle straight at a man, then suck back and race away from him again with incredible swiftness. They distorted figures and distances and perspective, but Will Duran, the half-breed Mexican, wasn't fooled by the heat; he was only annoyed by its heartless burning.

Fletcher saw him coming and halted out there, waiting. When Duran came up Fletcher said, 'Well; if you saw me I reckon others did too.'

Duran wiped off sweat with his limp sleeve. 'No; Cowdrey and his tame apes went into the saloon, Fletcher. They didn't see you. But if they'd stood outside another minute they'd have noticed you split off from the girl. Now what in the devil are you up to; if you think you can get that feller out of the...Say Fletcher; you didn't happen to keep the keys, did you?'

'Wish I had,' Markley mumbled. 'Will; I've got to talk to Harrison. That's why I slipped around here. To wait for nightfall, then sneak up, catch his jailer off-guard and get some answers from Harrison.'

Duran rolled his eyes with exasperation. 'Fletcher; they'd be after you like a pack of young wolves, if you busted into that jailhouse. Not only that, but they'll raise Cain if you so much as show your nose back in town again. Now listen to me, Fletcher; what is it you got to know? I'll go see Harrison and ask him, then I'll ride up to Arapaho's place and give you my answers.'

Fletcher looked wrathful and resentful. Duran saw that and adamantly wagged his head, re-stating all his arguments against Fletcher trying to go back into Evanston. He even added a few new arguments, just thought of, so in the end Fletcher agreed not to try it. Finally he said, 'Will; that boy may be an outlaw; I'm not going to deny that again. But last night when we were in the loft he could have gotten on his horse and ridden off. He didn't. He could've fainted or faked something wrong with him today instead of ridin' into town with us. He didn't do that either. Now I want to know exactly what's behind those charges against him up in Montana—then I want you to find out from him why he didn't slope when he could have. You got that?'

'Of course I got it,' snapped Duran, shaking off sweat again. 'Now you head for Arapaho's place an' as soon as I have the answers I'll come right on up. Maybe tonight; maybe in the morning. All right?'

Fletcher nodded and sat like a bitter-faced bronzed statue, glaring over towards the town. He said a harsh word, then turned his horse and loped back the way he'd come. He didn't even turn to glance back and see what Will Duran was doing. Somewhere far ahead, because he'd ordered her to go on, was Cynthia Whitson. She, like Fletcher himself, was not too much discomfited by the heat. They were used to it. Cynthia had never known anything different, and while Fletcher had, he'd nonetheless been in western New Mexico so long he'd almost forgotten there were cooler, greener places on earth.

And yet, when he swerved on his northward ride to head for the pool at Ute Creek, he found her already awaiting him there, and she was doing exactly what Fletcher had ridden over there to also do; she had her boots and socks off and was cooling her feet in the water.

When he came up, stepped down and left old Ned to stand in tree-shade or wander out gazing, as he chose, Cynthia said, 'What happened; you weren't gone long enough to see him in the jailhouse?'

'Will Duran rode out to talk me into letting him do it. He'll get what information he can, then he'll come up to the ranch sometime tomorrow.' Fletcher eased down, tugged his boots off, plunged his feet into the water and sighed with enormous relief.

'Can he do it?' she asked, gazing around at him.

'If Will can't do it no one can,' he replied, loosening all over and leaning his thick and heavy shoulders against the tree at their back. 'If those damned idiots had just given us a few minutes with him before they locked him up— but no—Frank Cowdrey's turning out to be just as big a tinhorn as Buster

124

also is.' He tossed down his hat, ran a set of bent fingers through his matted shock of hair, and looked at her.

She smiled at him. 'We'll win,' she murmured. 'You'll see, Sheriff. And Howard is no more an outlaw than I am. You'll see.'

She turned back towards the creek and he sat gazing at her profile. He was a lot older; right this minute he felt as old as the Ute Peak range of mountains on their right. Faith in people was so seldom really warranted; so seldom repaid by honesty and decency. He cleared his throat and dug for his pipe. She lifted her face to him.

'You don't think I'm right?' she murmured.

'I *hope* you're right,' he retorted, and packed in the tobacco, lit up and vigorously puffed until he had a good head of smoke up, then he met her steely glance and softly smiled. 'Sure you're right,' he said. 'We can't *both* be so wrong about Howard.'

She dropped her head again, watching the water run past. For a long while neither of them moved or spoke, then Fletcher heard something and straightened up to gaze around. A horseman was jogging towards them from southward, down in the blurry heat-haze. It wasn't Will, he could make out that much, and it wasn't Cowdrey or Munzer of Jack Phipps, because this man rode with the light hand and relaxed frame of a lifelong horseman. Finally, when Cynthia had also studied the approaching man for a moment, Fletcher recognised him.

'Flint Manly,' he said, and puffed on his pipe to keep it going.

Manly was a man older than Fletcher Markley. He was as lean as a stripling youth and as seamed and lined in the face as a watershed mountainside. He had pale blue eyes that made a startling contrast to his sun-darkened, oily hide, and when he smiled he showed worn, even strong teeth. He was the largest cow-calf man in the Evanston country; employed seven full-time riders and ran somewhere in the neighbourhood of twelve thousand cows.

Flint Manly was a rich, shrewd, tough old string of rawhide. He was mightily respected and because he was taciturn, in some quarters he was also feared. He never said a word he didn't mean, and he never used words he didn't have to speak. As he reined up now, barely within the shade of the tree where Fletcher and Cynthia sat, gazing upwards, he smiled at them, gallantly brushed the brim of his hat to the girl, and said, 'Fletcher; they made one hell of a mistake down there in town, yesterday. They made an even bigger one in the man they chose to replace you. I've known Buster Munzer since he first hit this country and went to work ridin' for me. He doesn't have it. He'll never have it. Today I heard some of my men were involved with him against you over at the Whitson place. Thought I'd ride up this way lookin' for you to say those cowboys don't work for Broken Bow any longer—as of today. Any other of my men want to buy in on Munzer's side; they'll get paid off too. I told 'em that at noon. I don't know what's goin' on, but I know a good man when I see one. You'll have no more trouble from Broken Bow. You got my word for it.' Manly lifted his reins, nodded, and spurred back the way he'd come.

CHAPTER 8

They eventually meandered on back to the log house, with dusk settling. They'd lingered down at the creek-side pool until most of the heat was past. They hadn't done that because either of them feared the heat, actually. They'd done it because from the creek southward down across Broken Bow's range, they'd had an excellent sighting of all the country Will Duran would have to cross on his way up to the Whitson place.

But Will hadn't come, so they'd hidden their private anxieties from one another and had talked of other things as they'd headed on back. As they were putting up their animals at the barn Fletcher said, 'He'll come, Cynthia. Don't you fret about that; Will Duran'll show up in the morning.'

Fletcher was right, Will did show up in the morning. He put his horse in the barn and walked over to the cabin, whistling. It wasn't that Will was pleased or light-hearted, it was simply that he'd no wish to be pot-shotted from a window over there simply because he hadn't previously announced himself.

Cynthia offered to make breakfast for Will. He declined, saying he'd been chewing jerky all the way up-country, and before he'd left town, ahead of sunup, he'd guzzled down a half gallon of coffee.

The three of them sat out on the little front porch. It was getting hot again, but for another hour anyway, it wouldn't be uncomfortable under

Arapaho's old warped wooden over-head-awning.

'Well,' Duran began, lighting a foul little Mexican cigar as coarse and black as sin, 'I got to talk to Harrison an' it's goin' to be hard for you to believe what he told me.' Duran stopped speaking, critically studied his cigar, then lifted his dark eyes to Cynthia. 'Part of it, anyway. The other part's believable enough. He said to tell Cynthia he'd get out of there and come back up here despite all the two-bit functionaries down there in town.'

Duran smiled gently, then saw Fletcher turning impatient and said, 'That horse *did* come from that murdered bank messenger up in Montana. This is the part he told you was his personal reason for going after Bragg and the other one.'

'Gibson,' muttered Fletcher, wishing to keep the record straight. 'Only Gibson wasn't with Bragg in

Montana. Harrison told me that before he went down to Evanston.'

'That's right,' conceded Will. 'This Gibson feller got recruited later, on down the trail, by Bragg.'

'Then who was with Bragg up in Montana—Howard Harrison?'

'Well yes,' said Duran, and raised a hand to silence Fletcher when he saw the former sheriff getting ready to speak again. 'Now let me finish, Fletcher. Bragg came onto a drift-camp up there, where two rangeriders were camping, checking drifting cattle for a big cow outfit. One of the men in that camp was Howard Harrison. The other was his ridin' partner. Bragg was on the run. He threw down on Howard, took his horse, which was fresh, and went on. When Harrison came around he took the tuckered horse Bragg left and went after him. He told me he had no trouble at all trackin' Bragg over as far as a stageroad. There, he saw Bragg and another feller talkin' out in the roadway. He was mad, naturally, took out his carbine and charged 'em.'

'You mean it was Howard who shot—?'

'Damn it,' snapped Duran irritably. '*Will* you let me finish? No; Howard didn't shoot the bank messenger—Bragg did. But that was *after* the messenger had handed over his money sack. You see, according to Howard, who sat back in the trees watching those two for a spell before he charged 'em, Bragg didn't have his gun out at all. In other words—'

'Yeah, I see,' murmured Fletcher. 'Bragg and the bank messenger were pardners. The messenger helped Bragg set up the robbery.'

'Right. Then, when Howard busted out of the trees with his carbine blazing, Bragg drew his sixgun and didn't shoot at Howard; he shot the bank messenger. Probably so he wouldn't have to hand over part of the money later on. This is only guesswork on Harrison's part, but I figure it's pretty close to the truth. Anyway—that's how the Montana officials sort of figured the thing. Only they figured there were *three* of them: Bragg, the messenger, and Howard Harrison. They figured those three got in a big fight over division of the loot, and the messenger got killed. Now, there was one other factor; Harrison's drift-camp pardner was coming down a far slope and saw that killing. He also saw Howard chase Bragg with his carbine blazin'. He identified Harrison easily enough, and the Montana authorities, reconstructin' how all this might have happened, put a wanted description out for Harrison.'

Fletcher fumbled for his pipe, stoked it up and sat for a long time rocking back and forth in his chair and reviewing all this, testing it against his own knowledge of criminals and criminal events. Finally he said, 'I studied those telegrams last night. It could all be true except one thing, Will. That damned horse.'

Duran snapped his fingers. 'I forgot that. It's sort of involved for me; I'm not real good at this kind of thing. The horse belonged to the bank messenger. When Harrison busted out of the trees on Bragg's run-down critter, the horse was failing under him. He abandoned it out in the roadway, got on the messenger's horse, and that's the critter he was still riding when he got down into our country.'

Fletcher puffed, his eyes nearly hidden behind the droop of lids, and eventually he said, 'He could've told me all that.'

'He could have, sure enough,' agreed Duran. 'The reason he didn't, he said, was because when Cynthia said she'd brought a friend home with her, that first day, she called you "Sheriff". He knew the law was after him as much as it was after Carl Bragg. He told me he didn't want to have to go back and spend six months in jail and in courtrooms, because then he'd likely loose Braggs' trail for good an' all. Even when he found out you weren't a sheriff any more, he told me he was afraid you'd still feel like one if you knew he was wanted. On top of that, he said, he was so close to getting Bragg when you showed up, it would've set him back all over again.'

Cynthia said, 'Mister Duran; do you believe him?'

Will didn't hesitate. 'I believe him. You bet I do. I'm convinced enough he's tellin' the truth I sent my barkeep down to send a telegram to the Montana authorities outlining his story, and askin' for more background on him: Does he have a previous record; was he ever suspected of criminal acts before; who could vouch for him and—'

'Will,' exclaimed Fletcher, suddenly and harshly. 'You darn fool, Phipps'll get that telegram too.'

Duran turned a crafty smile upon Fletcher. 'Not by a long shot he won't, old friend. Evanston isn't the only town that's got a telegraph office. I sent my barkeep fifty miles down-country to send that wire. He's to wait for the answer, then return to the saloon with it and not let a livin' soul see it. I figure he'll get back to town late tonight. Maybe about midnight or thereafter, an' I figure to be on hand when he gets back. Then we'll have something to go on—either Howard Harrison's tellin' the truth, or he's shady enough to be right handy at manufacturing likely lies. In either case we'll know enough to go on from there.'

'Go where?' asked Cynthia. 'If he's innocent he'll still be in their jail.'

'Not for long he won't,' stated Fletcher, letting his pipe go out in his big hand. 'We'll get a writ and force them to release him.'

'You won't get any such writ in Evanston,' Duran stated.

Fletcher's answer was brusque and oblique. 'You didn't send your telegram from there, either, did you?'

For a moment the three of them sat in quiet contemplation. Whatever their conversation might have included once they spoke out again, was anyone's guess, for it never got started again while they were sitting there on the porch. A horseman coming up the dusty trail halloed long before he came into sight, which wrenched their attention away from the Harrison story to this new event, and they all sprang up, walked out away from the house where they could see down the

138

trail, and Cynthia said, 'It's Flint Manly leading a horse.'

Fletcher and Will Duran made out the rider also, but being less familiar, couldn't deny nor affirm Cynthia's judgement for another ten minutes, or until Manly got up close enough. By then they'd gone down to the log barn, which was where Manly would enter the yard and make his first stop.

Will stepped inside the barn, got his Winchester and returned to the yard, just in case. But it was Flint Manly all right. When he was entering the yard through the yonder trees Duran muttered a mild curse and pointed to the horse Manly was leading.

'That's that cussed stud-horse that bit me,' he said.

Fletcher looked. Manly was leading the beast on a loose rope, he didn't have the animal's head snugged up close the way most mounted men led stallions. 'Are you sure?' he asked.

Duran rolled his dark eyes and unconsciously rubbed his hip pocket, 'Am I sure? I got plenty of reason to be sure!'

'He probably thinks it's some critter Cynthia owns, then,' stated Fletcher, logically enough.

Manly rode on up and halted ten feet from the tie-rack out front of the barn. He nodded around, didn't seem at all surprised to find the saloon-owner from town out at the Whitson ranch, and held up the tie-rope. 'How about one of you boys tyin' this critter to the rack,' he said. There was a shot-loaded rawhide quirt dangling from his wrist. 'An' be a mite careful, he may look old, but he's a stallion an' he nips.'

Fletcher reached for the rope, drew the stallion up and made him fast. Will stood back until that had been accomplished then lowered his carbine, looking puzzled. Flint Manly stepped down, shot a jaundiced look at the old stallion and gave his head a little shake. 'Cantankerous old cuss,' he murmured. 'If I hadn't had a quirt he'd have chewed up my horse.' Manly pushed back his sweat-stained hat, looked at the three of them wryly, then said, 'Fletcher; you ever see that old devil before?'

Markley shook his head but Will Duran spoke up. 'I have. He belongs to that good-lookin' gal who took over John Whitly's store. She's his sister, come on from some place back in Nebraska when she received word of Whitly's killing.'

Fletcher, who knew Flint Manly, said, 'Why, Flint? What's wrong?'

Manly stepped into the shade, tossed his reins around the far end of the tie-rack and blew out a long sigh as he gazed all around the yard before answering. Then he said, in that minimal, quiet-tough way he had of speaking. 'Couple of hold-up men rode him hell for leather as far as my horse pasture, left him there and went on with a pair of fresh horses they stole from me.'

Fletcher's expression never altered. He kept staring straight at the cowman. Will and Cynthia, however, showed shock and incredulity in their faces. Fletcher said, 'Go on, Flint. What's the rest of it?'

'They hit the general store down in town,' replied Manly, turning the full force of his steady gaze upon Fletcher Markley. 'The same two who tried it before, so they say, only this time the lady opened old Whitly's iron safe and they cleaned it out. You know, Fletcher; I had six thousand cash dollars in that box. After John Whitly refused to hand my money over, I just naturally left it there. But it looks like those two renegades figured that there'd be someone new runnin' the store after they killed old John, and they figured whoever'd be runnin' it now, wouldn't forget what'd happened to John. They figured right.'

Will Duran groaned and slapped his thigh with his hat. The others gazed at him. 'Three thousand dollars I had in that safe,' he said.

Manly nodded. 'You've got plenty of company, Will. Seems like they got about twenty thousand of our dollars. Biggest haul in the history of Evanston.'

Fletcher's lawman instincts were functioning. 'Are you sure it was the same pair who hit the town before?' he asked Manly.

The rancher nodded. 'Several folks saw them. It was the same pair.' Then, as though Manly thought he knew how Fletcher's thoughts were running, he said, 'Fletcher; there's no sense in hiding it from you. Folks are sayin' if you'd stayed on their tracks after their first raid, they'd never have been able to get back to hit the town again.'

Duran growled. 'That's silly, Flint. They fired Fletcher before he'd had a good chance.'

But Fletcher said, 'They're probably right, Flint. But I just never even got close to them. I'm not blaming myself, entirely though. I've had that happen before. Professional outlaws don't just charge into a town on the spur of the moment, rob it, then trust to fleet horses to get away. They plan every move. Those men did that. I was convinced of it when I was hunting them.'

'Well maybe,' Manly said softly, 'but down in town folks are saying you didn't stay on their trail, Fletcher. They're sayin' you'd come back to town every night instead of keepin' after them.'

'That's how it looked all right,' agreed the former sheriff. 'Maybe I should've explained, Flint, that I was convinced those men never left the country; that they had a hideout somewhere in the mountains.'

Duran and Manly exchanged a long look, then Manly gravely nodded. 'They probably wouldn't have believed you, Fletcher, but you know somethin'? I do. I believe you right now. Those damned thieves didn't come a long way to hit us this time. Folks said their horses weren't hardly sweatin' at all.'

Cynthia looked at Fletcher Markley. 'Sheriff,' she said. 'Do you think...?'

Fletcher was nodding, so she didn't finish it, his round face smoothed out and was thoughtful. 'Likely,' he said. 'Very likely, Cyn.'

'What's likely?' demanded Duran.

'That they headed straight back for their close-by hideout,' answered Fletcher. 'That they didn't leave the country this time either, and that they don't figure to, until all the uproar dies down like it did when they killed John Whitly.'

Manly and Duran and Cynthia Whitson regarded Fletcher Markley with a faint glimmer of hope in their eyes.

CHAPTER 9

Fletcher had an idea, so he asked Flint Manly about the route the outlaws had used leaving Evanston. Manly's answer was perfunctory. 'They headed north up the road for a mile or such a matter, then cut off westerly straight as a pair of arrows for my horse pasture. They roped two horses, left this snuffy old stud-horse and another stolen critter, and headed almost due north again, as far as I followed their tracks before splitting off to come over here and leave the stallion. I didn't want him loose with my mares and I didn't have time to take him all the way back to my home-place.'

Fletcher scratched his head. 'Something,' he said, 'doesn't jell here. Why did they steal two horses down in town?'

No one had an answer to offer, so none of the others said anything. Fletcher felt around for his pipe, stoked it and lit up again. He puffed and gazed at the stallion a while, then turned on Will Duran. He told Will to head on back to town and pick up all the information he could, then wait around for that telegram they'd discussed earlier, get some rest, and sometime after midnight to head on back to the Whitson place.

'If I'm not here,' he said, 'someone will be, an' they'll bring you to wherever I am.' He looked long at Duran. 'Will; be mighty careful down there. Munzer and his friends know you're a friend of mine. They're probably all fired up over this robbery.

You open your mouth at the wrong time and they'll stir up the whole blessed town against you.'

Duran said grimly, 'I'll be careful all right,' and went after his horse. Flint Manly stood eyeing Fletcher, but it was Cynthia who spoke next. She asked if Fletcher proposed riding over onto Broken Bow range to pick up the tracks of the robbers where Manly had left them. Fletcher agreed that this was his intention, but he also said, 'Only this time, Cynthia, I'm not just going to track them. I'm going to trick them.' He looked at her. 'I'm going to trick them if I can, anyway, an' if you like you can come along.'

Manly walked over and took loose the reins of his saddle animal. To Cynthia he said, 'Mind if I put this stud-horse in one of your back corrals by himself?' She shook her head; she didn't mind. Then Manly turned, stepped into his stirrup, rose up over leather and looked at Fletcher. 'Sheriff; what you got in mind for me?' he asked, and grinned as Fletcher looked up, also grinning. They understood one another, these two capable, older men.

'I'm going to take Cynthia out there on your range in broad daylight,' explained Fletcher, 'and we're goin' to make a big show of following those tracks. Then we're going to lose them up near the forest, Flint. We're going to lose 'em before sunset, out in plain sight of anyone watching from higher in the hills. We're then going to start down-country like we're heading back to town.'

'All right,' agreed Manly. 'And—me?'

'You're not going home from here. You're going over to the stageroad, stop the northbound afternoon coach, and tie your horse on the tailgate and buy passage over the mountains.

On the far side you'll cut back southward again, coming down behind them.'

Flint Manly shook his head. 'Not alone,' he said. 'Fletcher; if they downed me they could get clean away. I'd be the only man between them and escape out the far side of the mountains. But I know some pretty good passes through the mountains from Broken Bow. If I've got until tomorrow morning to accomplish it, I can ride home, round up my crew, push along all night and be far behind them by sunup. Then, with eight of us strung out, we can come down behind 'em neat as a whistle. Even if they ambush us, they sure won't get all eight men. We'll push them straight back down here to you.'

Fletcher considered Manly's plan as Will Duran walked his horse from the barn, mounted it and reined over to the others. Finally, Fletcher said he liked Manly's idea better than his own, providing Manly was certain he could get through the mountains to cut off the outlaws' northward retreat.

Manly was confident. He straightened in the saddle asking someone to hand him the lead shank to the old stallion. Fletcher waved him off, saying to forget it and head on home, that Fletcher would take care of the horse.

Manly and Duran loped away together. Fletcher put a squaw-bridle on the biting old stallion and led him out back. He'd scarcely set him free inside an empty corral and closed the gate when Cynthia said someone was coming from off towards the stage-road, which was easterly, in a rig. He joined her around front to study this unusual event. The plain below Arapaho Whitson's place was perfectly level; adequate for wheeled vehicles, but where the forest-fringe began, and the only trail on into the ranchyard was, although it was amply wide for a buggy or wagon, it was rough and rutted; there hadn't been a wagon over it since Arapaho had died, and there hadn't been a top-buggy over it for a decade before that, if ever. Arapaho hadn't known many people who owned such elegant conveyances. Neither, for that matter, did his daughter or Fletcher Markley. There were some livery rigs down in town, and perhaps a half dozen people in the Evanston country owned buckboards, spring wagons, or runabouts, but this was a fringed-top surrey, dusty and well-used, but still almighty elegant for the Ute Creek countryside.

Fletcher and the beautiful girl stood in barn-shade watching as the driver of that rig saw the rutted roadway and hesitated only a moment before plunging right on up it, hitting chuck-holes, ruts, washboard-ridges, with high-handed abandon. There were two people in the rig; one, the driver, was a thick-shouldered man, the other one was a woman. Fletcher saw her hat flip off and fall into the backseat where the rig hit a particularly bad bump. He also saw the flash of red-gold, wavy hair.

The surrey finally spun out of the last bad spot, veered up into the yard behind its team of perfectly matched chestnut geldings, and began to slow a little as the driver saw Fletcher and Cynthia standing in front of the old log barn.

Where the surrey finally stopped, dust churned. The driver was one of Frank Cowdrey's daymen from the liverybarn. Fletcher recognised him right off. The passenger though, was a perfect stranger. Fletcher strolled forward on the off-side to assist her down. She wore a ruffled blouse and a rusty-coloured riding skirt. She was also booted for riding, and in the back seat of the rig was a complete riding outfit; saddle, bridle, blanket, lead-shank, and even one of those heavy-handled shot-loaded rawhide quirts. The minute Fletcher saw that quirt he guessed the rest, and offered his hand to the very handsome woman in the rig, with curiosity rising in him.

She smiled, brushed back a heavy lock of coppery hair and said, 'I'm sorry. I didn't have in mind such a dramatic ride into your yard. I'm Angela Whitly. You may have known my brother, John Whitly. He used to run the store down in—'

'Ma'am,' said Fletcher, giving his Longhorn moustache a fierce upward twist. 'I knew your brother very well. Only, I'd sort of guessed maybe his sister'd be older than you are. Maybe about—'

Cynthia sweetly interrupted, at the same time digging Fletcher savagely in his unprotected ribs with her elbow. 'Miss Whitly; please get down. I'm Cynthia Whitson. I live here. We all were very sad at what happened to your brother. If you'd care to come over to the house there's water and something cool to drink.'

Angela Whitly alighted on her side of the surrey as her hired driver alighted on the far-side, and tended the sweaty team, taking them over into the shade so they wouldn't get blistered. She had a friendly, warm twinkle in her eye for Cynthia, then turned and said, 'You must be Mister Whitson,' to Fletcher. It caught him unprepared, so he simply stood there.

Cynthia said, 'No; this is Fletcher Markley, and old friend of my father's and mine.'

Both Cynthia and Fletcher saw the shadow pass swiftly across Angela Whitly's countenance at the sound of Fletcher's name. Then it was gone, she nodded at Fletcher, continued to gaze at him a moment, and finally looked back at Cynthia.

'I'm looking for a seal-brown stallion,' she said. 'My store was robbed this morning very early back in town, and the outlaws afterwards took two horses from my corral out back of the store building. One of them was a gelding; I'll find him sooner or later, I suppose, but the other one was my old pet Morgan stallion.'

'He's here,' stated Fletcher, admiring the mature stature and beauty of Angela Whitly. 'He's out back in a corral.'

She turned and fixed Fletcher with that strangely bright and reserved look once more. 'I'm very glad,' she said. 'He brought me all the way from Nebraska after I learned of my brother's—murder—Sheriff Markley.'

Fletcher nodded; so that was it; she'd been pumped full of the loose talk down in town against Fletcher Markley, the former sheriff. He said, 'If you'd like I'll fetch him along an' tie him to the back of the rig.'

Angela looked around for her hired driver. 'That won't be necessary at all, Mister Markley. I brought along a driver to take the rig back for me. He'll saddle and bridle my stallion, I'm quite sure, then I'll ride him back.'

'As you like,' murmured Fletcher, and started around the rig to where the liveryman was standing in barn shade. 'Come on,' he said to the hostler. 'Let's go get him.'

Fletcher paused in the barn doorway to watch Cynthia and Angela Whitly cross towards the house under the fierce, hot sun. The hostler grinned, reading Markley's thoughts. 'Ain't she somethin' to look at,' he said, strongly admiring. 'An' by golly she ain't married, Sheriff. Never been married, neither, so that old man who crossed the desert with her from Nebraska told us fellers at the saloon the other night. She had a big store back in Nebraska her uncle left her. She's been runnin' it most of her life, that old gaffer told us. Then she sold out and come down to Evanston when she got word of what'd happened to old John.'

Fletcher said, 'John Whitly was close to sixty. That woman's no more'n a bare forty. I just naturally thought a sister of Whitly's would be at least fifty or fifty-five.'

The raffish liveryman chuckled. 'I know. You ought to see the cowboys and unmarried townsmen wearin' out the plankwalk in front of old Whitly's store since she come to town. Why; I'll bet you the boys've bought enough sacks of tobacco they ain't needin' to patch hell a mile.'

Fletcher waited until Cynthia and the beautiful sister of old man Whitly passed from sight inside the log house over yonder, then grunted at the hostler and led the way out back where the stud-horse lay back his ears and bared his teeth at sight of them.

The hostler cocked his head to one side, studying that corralled animal. 'Say,' he drawled. 'Is this the spoilt old cuss she figures to ride back to town?'

Fletcher didn't answer. He studied the horse a moment, then tugged off his shell-belt, carefully laid aside his ivory-stocked sixgun and went inside the corral. The stallion rushed him, head and neck out to bite. Fletcher stood his ground until the very last moment, then swung. That shell-belt was heavy as lead, with its close-packed row of looped shells. It cracked down across the old horse's tender muzzle with a lot of force behind it. The stallion gave a loud snort, checked his fierce rush and whirled to get away. Fletcher swung one more time. The blow caught the ornery old cuss flush down across the rump. He sucked his tail under and jumped eight feet away. That was the end of it.

Fletcher methodically put his belt back on, dropped the forty-five back into place, took the bridle from the liveryman and ambled on over. The stallion rolled his eyes in fear, put his head down and let Fletcher bridle him without another hostile movement. When Fletcher turned his back and started for the gate, the old stud-horse followed him as meekly and obediently as a puppy. He'd made his customary challenge and his nose and rump still smarted from what had ensued; like nearly all spoilt horses, he was far too smart to push for a real battle, because, again like most spoilt horses, he really wasn't mean, he was just too pampered, too petted and wilful.

They took him around front, flung the blanket and saddle on him, and Fletcher deliberately cinched him too tight. For a second he almost forgot himself; he laid his little ears back, fiercely rolled both eyes and bared his teeth as though he meant to whip his head around and nip. Fletcher's big fist met him halfway, flush on his tender nose again. The ears came straight up, the eyes instantly lost their fierceness and began watering. That hadn't been a light tap on the nose.

Fletcher then loosened the cincha, re-set it properly and ran his big rough hand up the old horse's neck, lightly tugged at one ear, and gave the stallion a masculine slap of friendship. The old horse stood perfectly still until he dared roll his eye around where he could see Fletcher, then he understood exactly. They could become friends; it all depended on the horse. The old stallion put his head around and gently nuzzled Fletcher. They were friends.

The liveryman broadly smiled. 'You've handled a spoilt one or two in your day,' he said admiringly to Fletcher. 'It's worth seein' a man who knows when to hit 'em an' when not to.'

Fletcher didn't comment. He took the old horse over into shade of the barn, hunkered with his back to the logs and dug for his pipe. He was gazing across at he log house where the beautiful girl and the very handsome woman had disappeared. Finally he said, without looking at the liveryman at all, 'Go ahead; take the rig on back to town. I'll see that Miss Whitly gets started back all right.' As he lit his pipe and watched the hired driver go forward and untie the fine-harness team, he said, 'Is there a posse out after those outlaws?'

The hostler answered without looking around. 'Yeah. Sheriff Munzer took thirty men about a half hour after the robbery, and went out to track 'em down.' The liveryman set the checkreins, walked down and got into the rig, then flicked his lines and said, 'Sheriff; if Munzer finds them two I'll eat my hat. It's not like you was the law any more. What we got now is a would-be sheriff. *Adiòs.*'

CHAPTER 10

When Cynthia and Angela Whitly came across the yard again, Fletcher was still over in front of the barn in the shade, with the stud-horse drowsing complacently beside him. The old horse cocked one eye open at the sound of those two oncoming women, studied them a moment, and started to flatten his ears. Fletcher looked at him and growled in his throat. Both ears jumped straight up again. Just for a second there, the stallion had forgotten himself again.

Angela Whitly seemed different towards Fletcher when she and

Cynthia came over beside him in the shade. She looked at her old stallion and asked if he hadn't tried to bite. Fletcher lay a big hand alongside the stallion's neck and smiled down into the very handsome woman's eyes.

'We understand each other,' was all he said, and handed her the reins. She took them, still studying Fletcher. Cynthia looked from Fletcher to the handsome older woman, then turned abruptly, saying she had to go saddle her horse, and walked on into the barn.

Fletcher said, 'Ma'am; I can guess all the bunk you've been told about me. Maybe it's partly my fault, all right. But there's a heap of difference between a young man full of impatience and an older man who knows when to ride hard, and when not to.' He softly smiled at her. 'But there's one thing I'd sure like to know, and maybe you could explain it to me; at least you were down there this morning.'

'Ask it,' she said, watching his bronzed face. 'I'll certainly tell you if I can, Sheriff.'

'Why did those two outlaws take your horses after the robbery?'

'Oh,' murmured Angela Whitly, 'I understand what you're thinking. Well; they came to town late last night on the stage, Sheriff. We found that out this morning after the robbery. The reason they did that, folks said, was because they couldn't have possibly ridden back into Evanston after what they'd done before, without being recognised. They came on the stage in the darkness, had half the night to catch and saddle two horses—and probably chose my two out back because they were handiest to the store —then, after the robbery, they raced out of town before anyone even knew they'd come back again.'

Fletcher pondered this, found it acceptable, and offered his hand as Angela Whitly turned to mount her stallion. She let him assist her although he saw at once that she was an accomplished horsewoman. It was evident in a number of little ways which perhaps no one but another seasoned horseman would have recognised. As he stepped back he lifted his hat to her. Just for a moment she seemed undecided about something, then leaned swiftly and said, 'Mister Markley; now I can see first-hand just how ridiculous those stories are they've been telling me down in town.' She whirled the stallion, lightly rowelled him and loped easily out of the yard.

He was still standing out there looking southward, down across the heat-blurred southerly range when Cynthia came out leading two saddled horses, and pushed the rein of one animal into his fist. When he looked around, she smiled at him, said not a word, and mounted her animal.

They left the yard by way of the trail, but only followed it half way along. Fletcher cut off through the trees. When Cynthia inquired about this he just shrugged his shoulders and kept on riding. The beautiful girl was going to find out for herself that Fletcher Markley sitting on her front porch rocking and smoking, was an altogether different man from Fletcher Markley on a hot trail.

He didn't utter a word until they were almost two miles westerly, then he pointed out across the southward, bitter-bright land, and said, 'We should cut their sign onward a little ways, so we might as well go down there now, then hunt the sign.'

That's what they did. By the time Fletcher saw the tracks though, it was fiercely hot. Their animals walked head-hung, sweating profusely although they never went any faster than a plodding walk.

Fletcher had his hatbrim pulled so low above his keen eyes he had to lift his entire head to see out. He showed her where the outlaws had roped two fresh beasts, re-saddled, then had sped on. Later, he also showed her where Flint Manly had caught the stallion, had done a little tracking for himself a short distance, then had turned off to head for the Whitson place. After that, though, there were only those two sets of hurrying tracks to see, and nothing more passed between them.

Fletcher rode slowly. He'd stop at the slightest pretext. He dawdled and sweated and once he turned his face towards Cynthia and winked. 'If they're watching their back-trail, and outlaws almost always do, I wonder what they're thinking of a bumbling old fool who goes floundering around like this, and takes girls outlaw-tracking with him.'

She had the curt answer. 'They'll be thinking you're not the least bit dangerous to them.'

'I'm not,' he conceded, and winked. 'I'm just the bait. You too. The real work's being done by Flint Manly, and if he fails it'll be the first time he ever failed at anything in his life, to my knowledge anyway.'

They suffered from the draining heat, though, as also did their animals, so their sense of accomplishing something was minimised. Then Cynthia began having reasonable doubts. 'They wouldn't really risk hiding out within sight of town, would they, Sheriff?'

Fletcher didn't get a chance to reply. They were in close to the forested uplands now. Too close, actually, if they were being watched from farther up-country, to still be seen. This was approximately where Fletcher had meant to turn back and start his visibly dejected ride back southward as though he were giving up and heading for town again. but off to his right, passing in and out of the trees as though they were coming from the direction of the Whitson place, were four horsemen.

Cynthia didn't spot them until Fletcher warned her to be quiet, that thus far they hadn't been seen, but very shortly now they would be; those four riders were slouching along straight towards them. Fletcher dropped his right hand down, eased off the leather tie-down to his sixgun, and strained to make out the identity of those oncoming horsemen. Finally, when the four riders passed silently across a clearing spongy with pine-needles, he grunted. The leading rider was Buster Munzer. The second man was 'Pinky' Maddon, the third one was Frank Cowdrey and the last man, riding as though in extreme discomfort, was Jack Phipps.

Cynthia saw them. She eventually also recognised them. She turned quickly, anxiously, towards Fletcher, but his features were already closed down in an expression of harshness towards those younger men. He swung off silently, drew forth his carbine, rested it across the saddle-seat, and when those four were within seconds of seeing Fletcher and Cynthia a few yards ahead of them he softly called: 'That's far enough. Keep both hands in sight and sit perfectly still!'

Munzer yanked back on the reins as though he'd been struck at by a rattlesnake. He and the others finally located Cynthia all right, because she was still astride and upright, but even after they saw Fletcher's horse and gun, they still didn't have too good a sighting at him because he was on the off-side of his mount, hunched forward a little.

'Drop your weapons,' he ordered them, and to lend conviction to his words, he cocked the carbine. That little sound carried easily in the hot hush which lay all around.

Munzer started to say something. Fletcher swung his carbine straight towards the younger man. Munzer sat poised, as though he might still say whatever it was he had in mind. But the rock-steady barrel of that Winchester prevailed; Buster drew forth his gun and dropped it. The others followed his wise example.

'Now get down,' Fletcher said. They all four obeyed that order without any hesitancy. Now Fletcher stepped around his horse where they could all see him plainly enough. He eased down his carbine hammer, held the weapon up and told Cynthia to keep them covered; that if one of them so much as moved a finger, to shoot to kill.

Cynthia as well as the four younger men over there in forest-shade, red-faced, uncomfortable, humiliated, were totally at a loss about what Fletcher Markley was doing. He didn't long keep them that way. He handed Cynthia his sixgun, too, then walked on over to Buster Munzer. The bandage was still visible under Munzer's hat. The younger man winced from the older man's cold look. Fletcher reached over, flicked the badge Buster was wearing, said something Cynthia couldn't hear, and stepped on past to 'Pinky' Maddon. Here again, though, Fletcher's contempt held him back. But Frank Cowdrey, the one who'd scorned Fletcher back in town, ordering him out of Evanston, didn't earn that contempt. And Cowdrey seemed to know what was coming, because the moment Fletcher moved on him, Cowdrey side-stepped, raised both fists and swung.

Fletcher didn't have time to completely get clear. The fist grazed his cheek and knocked off his hat.

Fletcher stopped and smiled. 'One of you has enough guts,' he said and launched himself straight at Cowdrey. There were several inches difference in height between them, which wasn't perhaps critical, but Fletcher was a thickly put-up man while Frank Cowdrey was lithe and lean and panther-quick. He didn't dare let Fletcher get hold of him and Cowdrey knew that as he whipped left and right avoiding the older man's rushes. He also stung Fletcher with lightning-like little jabs from his left hand, then his right hand. He fought well, and if he was fearful or desperate, he didn't show it until just before he made his fatal mistake. After that it was too late to show anything.

Fletcher absorbed all those little stinging blows, settled back finally, feinted Cowdrey, and when the younger man went in, Fletcher whirled and caught him flush over the heart. Cowdrey wilted. His jaw dropped and his eyes rolled up. He lowered both hands. Fletcher moved in slowly and precisely, first with a sledging left, then with a blasting right. Frank Cowdrey went down, rolled several times and lay perfectly still.

Fletcher stepped past and Jack Phipps, raising his horror-struck face, saw Markley moving upon him. Phipps began bleating for mercy. He quavered and shook, holding out both arms in abject supplication. Fletcher halted and waited until Phipps's bleatings dwindled, then he turned and gazed back at Munzer and Maddon. 'Where are the others?' he asked. 'You left town with thirty men, this morning—Sheriff.'

Munzer made a vague, disconsolate gesture. 'I split them up into groups.

Some are over east of the stageroad, some are southward below town in case those damned outlaws cut back, some are—'

'And you,' growled Fletcher. 'Where were you going just now?'

'I was heading westward. It seemed likely they just might try getting away over in that direction.'

Fletcher walked back to confront Munzer. 'I'll tell you which way they went,' he said. 'The same damned direction they went that other time. Northward up through the mountains.'

Munzer rolled his eyes, looked around, then looked back again. 'Listen,' he said to Fletcher. 'I found somethin' out after that robbery this morning, Sheriff. I made a real bad mistake talkin' everyone into blamin' you for not getting them the other time. Sheriff Markley; I'll give you back the badge. You take over and lead us up where they went.'

Fletcher balefully regarded Buster Munzer. 'I've got a better idea,' he growled. 'You boys get on your horses and get out of my sight. You turn my stomach just lookin' at you. And Buster—I hope you don't find those killers. Not with what you've got with you today. Punks! Look at Phipps! You figure to fight it out with two professional gunmen with something like that along with you?'

Fletcher turned, walked back and took his pistol back from Cynthia, holstered it and reached for his carbine as well. He booted the Winchester, scooped up his reins and moved in close to mount up. Across the seat of his saddle he shot one final scornful look at the possemen with their sheriff over there in tree-shade.

'This is what Evanston wanted instead of me,' he said, swung up and settled across his saddle. 'The only thing I can think of is—Evanston deserves you, Buster.'

He turned his horse, gestured for Cynthia to come, turned and rode back out into the hot sunlight, which was now beginning to redden somewhat off in the west, where the sun was fast descending.

He rode along, smoky-eyed with indignation and powerful disgust without saying a word, for nearly a half hour, or until he was certain any watchers up in the higher country would get the idea that he was defeated at his tracking and was heading back for town, then he said, 'You think I was hard on them, Cynthia?'

She didn't answer right away. Eventually, though, she said, 'If you'd hit them all, Sheriff, I'd have thought you were. In fact, I'd have thought you were mean and being a bully. They just aren't in your class at all.' She twisted to look back. There was no sign of those four men back through the trees. As she straightened up she was smiling. 'Still,' she told him, 'I was hoping a little you'd do it anyway.'

He seemed to feel better after she told him that and smiled at him. He stoked up his pipe, lit the thing and rode down through the twilight towards the town relaxed and evidently satisfied with what he'd said and what he'd also done back there. When the shadows came puddling, though, he knocked out his pipe, pocketed the thing and turned brisk again.

'Now; you head on home,' he said to her. 'And you wait for Will. He'll show up at your cabin sometime between midnight and sunup, I'm pretty certain. When he does, you two meet me about a mile or two south of where we are right now. That's where I figure to lie down in the grass, come sunup, and pray to the good Lord that Flint Manly's flushed those two and started them out of the hills down towards me.'

She was sceptical. 'But suppose they're run out of the hills before we get back here to you?'

He shook his head, squinting at the darkening sky. 'Not a chance, Cynthia. Not a chance. But you two get right on back before sunup, or I'm goin' to have my hands full. All right?'

She nodded at him. 'All right, Sheriff,' she murmured, turned and rode off in an easy lope through the gathering early evening.

CHAPTER 11

Fletcher rode until there was no longer any possibility of anyone in the uplands seeing what he was doing because of the settling dusk, then he turned around and rode back up about to the spot where he'd been when he'd sent Cynthia back. There, he stepped down, drew forth his carbine, and made himself comfortable in the curing, tall grass.

There was a scent of cattle in the stillness, and a dry-hot odour from parched earth and cooling brush. Later, when a vagrant low breeze came down-country, he also picked up the pleasant smell of pine-sap.

He went over their plans in his mind,

found plenty of loopholes for things to go wrong, and wanted to light his pipe but didn't because the smell would travel too far.

His horse snuffled in the grass, dragging its reins. Old Ned was accustomed to these little lonely interludes and accepted them phlegmatically, making the most of whatever opportunity they offered to fill up on roughage. In this particular place, the opportunities were excellent.

It was just before nightfall finally settled that Fletcher picked up the soft-distant sound of an oncoming rider. He listened long enough to ascertain that the stranger was alone, then stood up out of the grass and tried to see him. He failed. The stars were out, as always, but that watery moonlight still hadn't firmed up enough to aid visibility very much.

He cradled his carbine and placed the direction of the night-rider, then began walking over in that direction, more curious than anxious. One thing he was quite positive that night-rider was *not*, was one of the wanted men up in the hills.

It occurred to him that this might be Will Duran, for some inexplicable reason coming north a good four or five hours before he'd expected to. It also occurred to Fletcher that it might be someone from Evanston; perhaps one of Buster Munzer's possemen. It never once crossed his mind it might be that man it turned out to be.

He saw the horse first, finally, because he was a flea-bit grey in colour; a very poor shade of animal for a night-rider to employ if he wished to avoid detection. He knew just about every horse in town, and quite a number of the ranch animals, but this flea-bit grey was new to him. There weren't many that colour in the country. It was not a popular colour anywhere west of the Missouri.

He dropped to one knee, leaning upon his Winchester, watching. The oncoming horseman was sitting erect and watchful. He rode with the air of a man either on the run or at the very least, desirous of avoiding contact with other men. That was good enough for the ex-sheriff. Whoever he was, beyond a doubt he was on the dodge. Fletcher stood up, waited until the horseman was less than three hundred feet away and gazing in the opposite direction, then he took several thrusting strides forward and raised his carbine.

'Stop where you are!'

The minute Fletcher said that the other man's right shoulder dropped. His right elbow flexed. He whipped his head back around, saw he'd never make it, that Fletcher's carbine was sighted squarely on him, and stopped both his horse and his dive for the gun he wore, at the same time.

Fletcher raised his head a little. There was now enough moonlight augmenting the starshine to make out features this close. He looked and blinked, and slowly lowered his saddle-gun. 'Boy,' he said softly, 'you'll never come any closer to it than you did just now.'

From the saddle, Howard Harrison said, 'I reckon you're plumb right, Sheriff, but if you'd turned out to be one of *them,* believe me, you'd have ridden right on down to the gates o' hell with me.'

Harrison stepped stiffly off the flea-bit grey, turned and led the animal on over. Fletcher relaxed slowly. 'How'd you get out?' he inquired.

'It wasn't as hard as you'd think,' replied the younger man. 'Even with a wound. They had an old man guardin' the jailhouse. This evening he proposed a game of whist. He sat outside and I sat inside. We played with the bars between us until I dropped my cards, outside.'

Fletcher said in a grating tone of voice, 'You don't have to finish, Howard. That's the oldest trick in the book. No one but an old man, or a total damn fool, would fall for it.'

Howard shrugged. 'Well; *he* did. I choked him down with my good arm, lifted the keys off him, walked out and borrowed his darn grey horse. They had my gun hangin' on a peg.'

'Obliging of 'em,' growled Fletcher, thoroughly disgusted. 'Well; there's a flock of them around us, but they won't make a contact as long as we keep on our toes and the darkness holds.' Fletcher then explained what he was doing out there, what Flint Manly and his Broken Bow riders were doing, and he also said what he hoped would be the outcome of all this. What he did *not* mention was that Will

Duran would be along sometime between midnight and sunup, with some factual background material on Howard Harrison, himself.

The younger man inquired about Cynthia. Fletcher explained where she was and why he'd sent her back. He also said, when Howard brought forth a tobacco sack, that the smell of a burning pipe or cigarette travelled miles on a clear, warm night.

Howard returned the tobacco sack to his pocket, lifted out the sixgun he wore, checked its cylinder then holstered the thing when Fletcher asked if he'd been followed out of town. He hadn't. Or at least as far as he knew, no one had seen him slip out of the jailhouse and depart from town on the flea-bit grey, because he hadn't gone straight up the north roadway, he'd cut around and departed to the west, out across Broken Bow range.

'Then,' said Fletcher, 'it's got to be

something else.'

Howard look up quizzically, as though he might ask a question. Off to the east a shod horse struck gravel, the discordant, low sound of that granite against steel carried perfectly in the hot night. Howard never had to ask his question. He whirled, reaching for his sixgun again, but Fletcher caught his upper arm, said, 'Take that damned grey horse off to the west a ways and keep him out of sight—along with yourself,' and gave a little push.

Howard turned back ready to protest, but Fletcher scowled and peremptorily gestured. The younger man moved, finally, caught the flea-bit grey and led it swiftly out through the murky night. Fletcher scarcely breathed for fear Howard's 'borrowed' horse would scuff up some noise, but through some kind of miracle, he never did.

Fletcher thought the oncoming

horses probably belonged to part of Buster Munzer's posse. That didn't especially bother him except that it was a trifle annoying having all these riders criss-crossing the plain. Unless they gave up and returned to town before sunup, when the Broken Bow men finally drove those two outlaws down out of the northward mountains, there was a very good chance someone was going to get shot, possibly killed, because Munzer's men didn't know what was going to happen; they were riding back and forth like sleep-walkers by now. They had been at it since early morning, it was now just an hour or two shy of midnight, and under those circumstances Fletcher Markley didn't expect them to be very alert, and they weren't.

He knelt in the tall grass to skyline them, then he estimated their course, figured he was safe from detection barring an accident, and then the 'accident' occured. The old flea-bit grey horse whinnied at either the sound or scent of those oncoming horses. Fletcher stifled a savage curse. The yonder possemen halted out in the darkness on the edge of visibility. Fletcher leaned upon his Winchester, mad as a hornet, waiting to see what they'd do. Someone out there said, hell, that had to be one of Flint Manly's loose horses. Another posseman agreed with that, then proposed they all turn southward and head for town. Another man grumbled thickly that he wasn't used to all this riding, and neither was his horse; on top of that, he thought they were being foolish, riding back and forth like this, because, since they'd cut no fresh sign all day long, the outlaws were un-questionably twenty miles away by now.'

Fletcher scarcely breathed. He was hoping his hardest those disgruntled possemen would prevail, and it seemed they had when the riders started moving again, because whoever was leading them angled around and struck out southward, down in the general direction of Evanston.

Fletcher kept them skylined from his low position out there on their distant right. Once, he turned to crane around, seeking some sign of Howard and that blasted grey horse. All they'd need would be for that critter to whinny again. It didn't happen, and eventually the last of those slumped riders passed gloomily down across the range, out of sight and eventually also out of hearing.

Howard walked back, leading the grey. Fletcher got to his feet, winced when all his weight fell upon his game right leg, turned a hard look upon the old horse and said, 'We'd be better off if you set that darned critter loose. He's going to get us into trouble yet.'

Far southward several men called sharply in the night. For a moment there was silence, then other men, probably the possemen who'd dejectedly headed for town, called back. Fletcher listened a moment, guessing what this was all about, then turned and jerked his head at the grey and repeated what he'd said earlier, but this time in a fully authoritative voice.

'Haul your saddle and bridle off that critter and set him free.'

Howard moved to obey, but he looked across his shoulder and said, 'What's it all about, down there?'

'My guess is that the first ones to yell were some fellers from town who're roiled up because by now everyone down there knows you've escaped. The second ones were those same men who passed us a while back. If the men from town can talk the other ones into it, they'll turn back and start scouring the damned countryside for you, this time, instead of those outlaws. If we're caught out here with that stolen horse...' Fletcher didn't bother to finish it. He didn't have to. Howard stripped the grey, led it off a little distance so that it wouldn't run over where Fletcher's horse was drowsing, then gave it a slap across the rump. The horse snorted, jumped as if hit by a hornet, and broke away southward in a belly-down run.

As Howard and Fletcher stood together out there where Harrison's tack lay in the grass, they could distinctly hear those possemen down upon the more southerly reaches of Manly's range raise several quick, sharp outcries at the sound of a running horse passing them to the west.

Fletcher took down a deep breath and let it out. 'He did us a favour, that cussed old horse. They're chasing him. Listen.'

Unaware that they were pursuing a loose horse, those excited possemen down there were rushing in the wake of the flea-bit grey with whoops and hollers. Of course the effect of such wild pursuit would only further frighten the grey horse. Those possemen would be lucky if they even got in sight of him by the time they got back to Evanston.

Fletcher wagged his head, felt around for his pipe, remembered the remonstrance he'd made when Howard would have lit up a cigarette, withdrew his hand and eased down in the grass with Howard ten feet from him.

Overhead, the moon was dropping away from its meridian. Elsewhere, the night was hushed and endlessly slumbering. Once, Fletcher thought he heard a twig snap, or a limb pop somewhere far off. He listened, heard a couple more of those faint, vague little reports, then resumed his restful position when they ended, finally, the silence closed in all around once more, and Howard Harrison asked if Fletcher was sure he could count on Flint Manly and his Broken Bow riders.

Fletcher said if he couldn't count on Flint Manly there wasn't a person on earth he *could* count on. After that for a while they lay back half drowsing. Old Ned, Fletcher's horse, ambled over to make certain he hadn't been abandoned out there, satisfied himself Fletcher was still close by, turned and ambled off again, all without once stepping upon his dragging reins. He was a wise old saddlehorse; he carried his head off to one side.

It was near two in the morning, according to Fletcher's closest reckoning, when they picked up the sounds of a loping horse passing far to their left, over to the east. They sat up listening. Fletcher thought that would be Will Duran out there, but when Howard volunteered to go over and make contact Fletcher shook his head. 'You'd never make it,' he opined. He was correct. Duran's horse was obviously fresh and willing. He passed on northward without a break in his stride. Within moments after they'd initially detected the sound, it was fading out again.

Fletcher considered a little nagging desire to light his pipe. He frowned it down, lay back again and mightily yawned. 'Howard,' he said quietly. 'If you'd told me how and why you got outlawed that first day at Cynthia's cabin, I have a feelin' between the two of us we could've prevented a lot of this from happening. At least I'd have taken you down to Evanston the day Whitly's store was robbed by your friends the second time, and with a little good aimin' and fast firin' I reckon we could've satisfied both of us.'

Howard was slow replying. 'Right or wrong,' he finally said, 'that's water under the bridge now, Fletcher.'

They didn't have much more to say for a while; each of them lay there watching the high sky, pursuing their own private speculations for a while. Then Fletcher said, 'Howard; did you see Miss Whitly down in town?'

'No; didn't actually see her, but I heard enough to *want* to see her. Even that old man they had guardin' me said she was the finest specimen of mature womanhood he'd ever seen. Why; have you seen her?'

'Today,' murmured Fletcher, curling his moustache. 'And by grabs as soon as we nail these outlaws I aim to see a lot more of her too.'

'You'll likely have to wait in line, from what I hear,' murmured Howard drowsily.

Fletcher's answer to that was a big, loud grunt.

CHAPTER 12

It was close to four o'clock without a noise anywhere, with old Ned standing hip-shot asleep, his lower lip fluttering, and with both Fletcher and Howard half asleep, when a distant sound came down the night to arouse both men.

It wasn't the rattle of gunshots nor the rush of shod horses so much as it was a reverberation which carried back and forth through quiet night-time air. Simultaneously with this presentiment which brought Fletcher up to a kneeling posture, Howard said there were two riders coming towards them from the northeast. Fletcher listened for this fresh sound, failed to pick it up right away, and turned back to try and discern what that other thing was which was also coming towards them out of the north-westerly night.

Howard got up, finally, settled the hat atop his head and asked if Fletcher could hear the oncoming pair of horses. Fletcher could hear them now, but he thought he knew who'd be riding those animals so all he did was grunt as he stood up, a trifle stiffly, and worked his game leg up and down to loosen its muscles and tendons.

'Go stop 'em,' he said to the younger man. 'It'll be Will Duran an' Cynthia.'

Howard walked off, moving swiftly across in front of Fletcher, sixgun in hand. He passed from sight a hundred feet onward, heading straight towards the sound of those slowing horses out there. Fletcher worked all the kinks out of his leg and examined his carbine. There'd been no dew in the night so the gun was still in excellent shape. He turned towards the north-west, straining to hear, annoyed with himself because secretly he'd noticed something lately—others heard things moments before he did. He tried telling himself that was only because other folks were listening when he was not listening, but it didn't go down. He finally shrugged off what seemed to be the truth about this small matter, and concentrated on picking up that troubled, far-off roil in the darkness which had initially aroused him from his half-sleep.

Someone several hundred feet off called to someone else. Fletcher recognised young Harrison's voice, then the deeper, rougher tones of Will Duran. After that he stood waiting until they all came back to him, still trying to detect the exact location of that other very vague, shifting sound.

Cynthia was wearing a fringed buckskin jacket the colour of new gold. Beneath it she wore a white blouse that shone in the darkness. Until he saw her sitting up there atop a horse, Fletcher hadn't thought much of the danger. Now he did. He also reflected, while the others greeted him, that if he'd let Howard take old Ned a while back and intercept Will when Duran was riding on up to the Whitson place, he could have stopped Will and in that way prevented Cynthia from being where danger seemed imminent, now.

But, as young Harrison had said earlier, that was so much water under the bridge; she was here, trouble was on its way, and even if he tried to send her back home, she probably would refuse to go, but whether she did or not, perhaps the safest place for her was right where she was. At least there were three guns to see that no harm came to her.

Duran dismounted stiffly and walked soberly up, dug out a piece of yellow paper and wordlessly handed it to Fletcher. He had to hold it up almost to his nose to make out the writing. To make certain, he re-read it, then in the same wordless manner handed it back. Duran said, 'Satisfied?' Fletcher nodded.

'Satisfied,' he said.

The telegram stated that Howard Harrison, up until he was outlawed on suspicion of complicity in a murder, had been highly thought of up in the Montana country. It also said he had no previous record as a criminal, and that there was considerable discontent among his Montana friends and former employers, about him being branded an outlaw on no more actual proof than had been offered against him.

While Will and Fletcher were standing close with that telegram between them, Cynthia and young Harrison were speaking together out where the horses stood, in low, soft tones. Fletcher looked at them a moment, started to say something, shifted his attention to Duran and said something else.

'You hear anything up north?' he inquired.

Will nodded, although at that precise moment the night was as still as it could have possibly been. 'Riders,' Duran said. 'Cynthia an' I heard 'em better when we were up there to the east.'

Fletcher nodded. 'Howard; you go off to the west a half mile or so. Use Cynthia's horse and keep your ears open. Will; you go with him. If that's what I think it is up there—Broken Bow flushing Bragg and Gibson down out of the mountains—we've got to guess where they'll come, and be there

206

in front when they come across this range.'

Cynthia walked up. 'I can go too,' she said. Fletcher shook his head at her.

'You stay right here with me. We're shy a horse, and if worst comes to worst, Ned'll carry the both of us well enough.'

For a moment his harshness, prompted by all that had happened this night, and what was certain to lie ahead, softened. He reached out and did an unprecedented thing. He lifted a heavy coil of her hair off one shoulder of the buckskin jacket and gently pushed it back, then he lowered his hand and quietly said, 'Cyn; there are an awful lot of young bucks in this world, an' maybe old Arapaho didn't do you any favour keeping you up at the clearing all these years. What I'm trying to tell you is that, if you'll take plenty of time you'll maybe be sure...You understand?'

She smiled up into his eyes. 'I understand,' she said. 'I understand why my
father used to tell me if I ever needed a
good friend and a wise one, after he
was gone, I was to go to you.'

Fletcher smiled back at her.

Duran came trotting up out of the
darkness excited and anxious.
'Riders,' he hissed at Fletcher. 'Sounds
like maybe two. They're coming
straight down towards the place out
yonder where I left Harrison. You'd
better get on that horse, Fletcher.'

Cynthia brought old Ned up and
held out the reins. She seemed to
understand what Fletcher wanted of
her because, as he reached, she said,
'I'll stay here, low in the grass.'

Fletcher mounted, nodded, and
whirled to ride back with Duran. They
didn't have far to go, no more than a
half or two-thirds of a mile, then they
both caught the sounds of horsemen
moving swiftly down across the north-

ward plain. Duran said, 'Now what?' and Fletcher eased out his ivory-stocked sixgun.

'Pray we're right,' he replied quietly. 'Get Howard over here. We'll try to hit them from this side as they go past.'

Duran returned in moments. Howard, riding Cynthia's horse, had his weapon palmed now in his lap as he reined in beside Fletcher. They sat like statues, listening to those oncoming riders. At the last moment Will had reservations. 'Suppose,' he whispered, 'it's Broken Bow.'

Fletcher shook his head. Manly wouldn't divide his men and have only two of them riding down here like this, in the first place, and in the second place, as he whispered back to Will, there were other horsemen coming, far back. If Will would listen close, he'd heard that other sound in the night.

Will listened but apparently heard

nothing. Howard did, though; he leaned far over and told Duran it sounded to him like a large body of mounted men strung out from east to west.

Fletcher gauged the gait of those invisible horses, decided it was time to move and grunted at his companions at the same time easing his horse forward. Old Ned walked stolidly; if he had any inkling of what impended he gave no sign at all of it.

Duran was on Fletcher's left, Harrison was on his right. Between the three of them there lay about twenty feet, give or take a few feet, dividing them. Fletcher had the sounds pegged perfectly. When he finally sighted blurry movement on his right, passing down from north to south, he raised his sixgun. The three of them were well within range now.

Duran and Howard Harrison did likewise.

Fletcher sucked in a big breath, hesitated until he was certain, then sang out. 'Stop where you are boys!'

It acted like a signal of some kind. Instead of obeying, the outlaws went for their guns. Fletcher saw that vaguely; two mounted men hunching down in their saddles. He didn't wait, he fired. One of the outlaws drunkenly yawed in his saddle. The other one blazed back and hooked his horse hard. As he swung even with the other horse, he swung his romal hard across the beast's rump. Both the horses sprang ahead in a wild jump and lit down running hard.

Will and Howard also fired, but the targets were veering off, seeking to put more darkness between themselves and their new enemies as rapidly as possible, so those two shots missed.

Now the chase began, punctuated by gunshots on both sides. Up north a carbine boomed, but Fletcher paid it no heed. Duran craned around, uncertain about the possibility that there might be additional enemies around them. For as long as it took him to do this, Will didn't fire. But Howard didn't look back at all; he was concentrating as hard as Fletcher also was on either overtaking their prey or shooting it out of the saddle.

Only one of the outlaws was firing, but he'd twist in his saddle and throw and occasional shot. Fletcher counted those bullets; when the sixth one had been fired he hooked old Ned hard and broke clear of Duran and Harrison, rushed almost up to the fleeing outlaws and yelled.

'Haul up those horses! I've got you both in my sights! Haul up or I shoot!'

The outlaw dead ahead was tugging out his carbine, sitting twisted in his saddle. He could see Fletcher less than a hundred feet back, sixgun up and cocked. For perhaps two hundred feet those two, hunted and hunter, rode along like that, then on ahead, closing in from the northwest, two riders shouted and shot. The bullets sang too close. The outlaw let go his carbine, straightened up and reared back on the reins. He'd had enough. His companion's horse shot ahead, unchecked. Fletcher let it go. He could've dropped the horse with one shot, but he didn't for the obvious reason that this second renegade was heading right out there where those converging Broken Bow rangemen were waiting.

Duran and Harrison roared up as Fletcher slowed beside his prisoner and growled for the outlaw to jettison all his guns. The outlaw didn't hesitate at all. Afterwards, he held both his hands up as high as his shoulders, palms forward. He was a thin-lipped, grey-eyed man with the stamp of cruelty across his long, narrow features. He looked at Fletcher, at Will Duran, and finally he looked longest at Howard Harrison. He seemed to recognise Howard, or at least to be struggling to recognise him, when on ahead someone fired a gun and roared a curse, simultaneously. They all heard those Broken Bow men sound off as they closed in like wolves around the second outlaw.

Fletcher holstered his sixgun and ordered the outlaw to dismount. As soon as he did this, Fletcher told Will and Howard to go over him inch by inch for a hideout-gun. They found a knife in the outlaw's right boot and an under-and-over nickel-plated .41 derringer inside his jacket, sewn into a special little buckskin sheath.

Fletcher dismounted. 'Which one are you?' he demanded. 'Bragg or Gibson?'

Howard answered. 'He's Carl Bragg.'

The outlaw turned, again trying to

place Howard Harrison. A look of astonishment suddenly broke over his cruel, narrow features. He said, 'I'll be damned—the Montana cowboy who loaned me his fresh horse.'

No one said anything. The Broken Bow rangemen were approaching at a slow walk. They had the other outlaw in among them. Flint Manly was out front. The moment he saw Fletcher he drew rein, jerked a thumb over his shoulder and said, 'This one's shot, Sheriff. We'd better ease him down onto the ground.'

Fletcher went across to assist in lifting the wounded man out of his saddle. He was thin and thirtyish with a rat-like pair of tightly-closed eyes and a grey, putty-coloured face. Fletcher's bullet had caught him high and to one side, ploughing through the outlaw's shoulder making a messy wound.

'That,' said Carl Bragg, without

being asked, 'is Hank Gibson.' He watched the cowboys put Gibson tenderly upon the warm ground and neither bent to examine his companion's wound, nor asked how bad it was.

Fletcher watched Flint Manly and two of his men go to work over the writhing, wounded man. Gibson was in extreme pain. The subsequent jolting he'd taken upon his running horse hadn't helped any. He groaned behind locked teeth as the cattlemen went to work staunching his wound and making a workable bandage from Gibson's filthy shirt.

Fletcher went back in front of Bragg. The two men exchanged a long look in complete silence. Bragg was tough and hard and uncompromising, that was immediately evident. He was captured, disarmed, and in the hands of men who'd be pleased to kill him on the spot, and he didn't bat an eye nor make a single cringing movement.

Fletcher turned away. 'Howard,' he said. 'You better get on over where we four were last together. Cynthia's waiting. Then we'll head for town.' Fletcher said that so matter-of-factly that even Flint Manly looked up from his bloody work. Fletcher moved over beside Manly, dropped to one knee and said, 'For old John Whitly's sake, I wish I'd hit eight inches more towards the centre.'

Manly nodded and returned to his work. Bragg swore when Will Duran produced a length of rawhide and roughly proceeded to tie the renegade's hands behind his back. 'Where the hell do you think I can go unarmed an' with a lousy army all around me?' he snarled.

Will went right on working as he said, 'To hell, mister, that's where you can go. And if I had my way you'd be on your way right this minute. Now shut up and quit wiggling!'

CHAPTER 13

It was a silent ride down to Evanston, or nearly so. Flint Manly sent all but two of his men on home when they were parallel with the trail leading to the headquarters ranch of Broken Bow. He also told Fletcher he'd like to go home, himself, and sleep for a week, then eat for another week. But when Fletcher told him to go on, head for home, Manly's dark, seamed face turned thoughtful and he declined. He didn't say why he wouldn't leave Fletcher and the others, though.

Cynthia and Howard Harrison rode on either side of Hank Gibson, with a Broken Bow rider behind and another one in front. They took turns steadying the wounded man, whose pain seemed to be constant and unnerving, although Gibson scarcely made any noise at all.

They were close enough to see the scattered outdoor night-lights here and there up and down Evanston's main thoroughfare, when Will Duran pulled in beside Fletcher on the left side—Manly was slouching along morosely on his right side—and said, 'This is going to make Buster and those other damned idiots look exactly like the tin-horns they really are, Fletcher. I hope they're still up and stirrin' when we ride down the roadway.'

But they weren't. No one was abroad in town as the grim, dusty, weary cavalcade headed down into town and passed ponderously along as far as the jailhouse, then stopped. There wasn't a soul in sight even down at Frank Cowdrey's liverybarn. It was close to sunup, though, which meant it was also close to the time when folks would be rousing themselves out of a long night's rest.

Fletcher crossed to the jailhouse door, heaved his weight to throw it back, and an old man sitting at the desk propped so far back his worn boot-soles were higher than his head, gave such a sudden start that the chair skidded from beneath him, hurling the jail-house-guard over backwards in a squawking heap of thrashing arms and legs. He'd evidently been sound asleep when Fletcher hit that door hard enough to send it violently around where it struck the log wall.

The old man rolled and flopped, got up onto all fours and stared pop-eyed as Flint and two of his Broken Bow men carried Hank Gibson inside. Then came Will Duran with Carl Bragg, and finally, the old man down on all fours, saw Howard Harrison, and went for his gun.

Fletcher leaned over, grasped the sixgun by its wavering barrel and forced it straight upwards. 'Let go of that thing,' he growled. The old man let go at once. Fletcher flung the gun across into a corner of his former office, picked up the jailhouse-guard by the scruff of the neck, stepped to the door and heaved him out into the dusty, soft-lighted roadway. The old man bounced to his feet and went flinging along up the centre of the roadway without uttering a sound but with his arms and legs pumping up and down.

Cynthia was over tending to the wounded outlaw. Someone had given Carl Bragg a tobacco sack. He was coolly manufacturing himself a smoke. Except for a low word now and then among the people in the cramped and crowded log jailhouse, there wasn't a sound anywhere.

Flint Manly strolled over, looked out the doorway, stepped back and said, 'Fletcher; that old man'll have Buster and his friends at your throat in twenty minutes.'

'They're not in town,' said Fletcher, reaching out to swing the door partially closed. 'At least the last time I saw the lot of 'em, they weren't. Cynthia and I ran onto them up in the foothills of your range, scouting through the trees.'

Manly wasn't convinced though, he looked out again, sucked his underlip a moment, then thoughtfully said, 'Maybe, if we left the wounded one here and all the rest of us went out to my place—just for the rest of the night, Fletcher...'

Carl Bragg strolled over and said, blowing out cigarette smoke, 'Old-timer; the way I've been piecing things together, you've got a tiger by the tail.

You dasn't hang on an' you dasn't turn loose.'

Fletcher turned and struck out in a blur of speed, knocking the cigarette from Bragg's lips without touching the man at all. 'Get over there,' he growled. 'The next time you talk, wait for someone to ask you to. *Move!*'

Bragg moved.

Cynthia had the Broken Bow cowboys helping her. She was a surprisingly handy nurse. Howard Harrison hovered nearby. Only Will and Flint Manly and Fletcher seemed concerned with other matters. Duran said, 'Fletcher; when Buster comes back he'll take over. We'll be damned lucky if he don't fling us all in jail, along with those two outlaws.'

Manly snorted. 'That'll be the day I'd like to see,' he growled. 'I wet-nursed Buster Munzer when he first arrived in this country. Frank Cowdrey too, for that matter. The day either one or both of those two put me behind bars'll be the same day hell freezes over.'

Out in the roadway several men called raucously back and forth. Flint Manly stepped ahead, pulled open the door and craned outward again. Without drawing back, this time, he said, 'Well; here it comes, Fletcher. An' you were wrong: Buster's back in town. He's comin' right now with some of his pardners.' Manly eased aside as Fletcher moved up for a look. The old cowman shook his head dolorously back and forth. 'Damn it, I'm slippin',' he muttered, as much to himself as to the others around him. 'Why didn't I keep all my men with us?'

It was a good question, but the answer was plain enough—painfully plain—when Fletcher pulled back inside and closed the jailhouse door: Manly hadn't, and that was that.

A man's gauntletted fist thumped upon the door at Fletcher's back accompanied by an angry voice. 'Open up in there! In the name o' the law, open that door! This is Sheriff Munzer; if you don't open that door I'll—'

Fletcher turned and suddenly yanked back hard on the door. Munzer plunged on inside. Behind him several startled cronies reared back when the bright orange lampglow struck them. Fletcher slammed the door and barred it from the inside.

Munzer blinked in the light, turning slowly from left to right. At sight of Howard Harrison he curled his lip in anger. 'Damn you,' he said, and got no further. Flint Manly reached out, spun Munzer by the shoulder and pushed his lean and leathery old face up close.

'Mind your language, boy. There's a lady in here. If you don't I'll just naturally carve out your gizzard and make it into a headstall for my horse.'

Munzer's colour mounted. He was already red-faced, red-haired and red-necked, so this was noticeable only to those who knew him best. He jerked away from Manly and turned again, full of angry defiance. 'You people listen to me,' he snarled. 'I'm the law here an' I say you're trespassing in this jailhouse. I also say you've interfered with the performance of lawmen performin' their legal duties. For that I'm goin' to lock the whole bunch of you up and throw away the key!'

Fletcher accepted a black cigar from Will Duran, leaned down for a light and afterwards deliberately blew a big gust of potent smoke in Munzer's direction, his face perfectly blank but his blue eyes smouldering. 'You pipsqueak,' he said softly. 'You're not goin' to lock anyone up but those two outlaws—which you couldn't find even though they were riding right down towards where I met you this evening.'

Munzer's friends outside, seemingly augmented now in their numbers and therefore bolder, began shouting and striking the jailhouse door. No one paid much attention to them until one man with a harsh, grating voice cried out that he had the rope and knew the tree where they'd hang Bragg and Gibson. He silenced everyone inside the jailhouse when he finished up that shout with: 'Buster; open the damned door. You know what you said—that you'd help us haul on the rope.'

Cynthia and Howard Harrison turned to slowly gaze over at Munzer. The pair of Broken Bow cowboys, along with Carl Bragg, Will Duran and Fletcher Markley were also staring at him. Bragg said, smoking another cigarette and looking straight through Munzer, 'Mister; if I'd figured it was a lynch-party waitin' down here for us, you'd have had to kill us out there on that plain.' He dropped the smoke and ground it out, lifted his cruel, hard grey eyes and said, 'An' mister; you're not goin' to do it now, either, without one hell of a fight. Set your mind to rest on that, 'cause a man only dies once, an' he's a heap better off kicking like a stallion when he goes out, than bleatin' like a lamb.'

'No one's going to get lynched,' said Fletcher, gazing at Munzer. 'Buster; if you think wearin' my badge gives you unlimited authority let me set you straight.'

'You go to hell,' snapped Munzer, and whirled to grasp the door-latch. Fletcher was there, anticipating that, with one big paw bearing down hard upon the latch-bolt. They were nearly toe to toe. Munzer said, 'Let go, Markley. Get clear of this door. I already got a warrant sworn out for you for what you done to Frank Cowdrey and Jack Phipps today. Aggravated assault. I found it in one of your own lousy lawbooks. Aggravated assault carries with it a minimum stretch in the pen of—'

'If you're joking,' said Flint Manly, 'it's stopped being funny. If you're *not* kidding, Buster, there's got to be something wrong with you in the head. Look around you here; the only two men in this room you don't know are these two outlaws. We tricked 'em and trapped 'em and they're going out of it. They lost, Buster, so now they stand trial and go to prison—or maybe the firin' squad or hangrope for murderin' John Whitly. But at least it's done. Look at me; you used to work for me. Look at Will and Fletcher and Cynthia and—'

'You know what I see,' exploded the red-faced wild looking younger man. 'I'll tell you what I see—a bunch of stinkin' hypocrites. You, Manly, with all that land and all them cattle and money. You're the worst. You stole the land from the redskins; you probably got your herds the same way. You, Duran; you been cheatin' folks on liquor to get rich over there in the *Claybank* since I been around here. And you, Markley; you're the worst of all, struttin' up an' down the roadway wearing this badge makin' folks kowtow to you. Wearin' that ivory-stocked pistol and limpin' along like a big hero …Well, by gawd; I brought you down, Markley; brought you down to nothin'. Rubbed your lousy nose in the dirt. Manly's next. Then all the others who've lorded it over me. One by one I'll break you an' humble you an'…' Munzer ran out of breath. He stood panting, glaring wildly around. No one said a word or so much as moved a foot or hand. Even Bragg was staring, looking stony-faced and mildly puzzled.

Munzer wrenched open the door, jumped through and slammed the panel after himself. For several moments after he'd departed no one in the jailhouse office said a word. Fletcher chewed upon the Mex cigar Will had given him, frowning at the floor. Manly and his riders looked back and forth.

Cynthia said, looking around at them all, 'Something *is* wrong with him. He didn't act—sane—just now.'

Fletcher eventually came down from his reverie and looking at Will and Flint, said, 'So that was it. I didn't know. It sort of had me worried. I knew he didn't like me, but I didn't understand how he'd undercut me, until I handed in my badge. But even then I didn't know why he and Frank Cowdrey did that to me.'

Manly said, 'All right, Fletcher, now you know. I'm as surprised as you are. He's got something gnawing away inside him. Like Cynthia said, he's not sane.'

Carl Bragg said, 'Yeah? Well now that you fellers have all that worked out, tell me somethin': If he's crazy how come him to have all them other fellers out there backin' him? Are they crazy too? Don't answer; it'd be a waste of time. What you fellers better concentrate on now is how you're goin' to prevent 'em from gettin' in here to lynch me'n Hank. You took us. We're your responsibility.'

'Oh shut up,' one of the Broken Bow cowboys growled at Bragg. 'If you could've used your lousy tongue instead of a pistol to get rich, Bragg, by now you'd be a millionaire.'

Fletcher went over to stand towering over Cynthia gazing at the wounded man. He was as white as a ghost but some of the bulging tautness had left his jaws; he was no longer clenching his teeth and from time to time he'd open his eyes. He did that now, saw Fletcher looking gravely down at him, and blinked.

'You the law?' he husked.

Fletcher said, 'Why, Gibson?'

'I got somethin' to tell you.'

Fletcher eased down, his thick shoulder touching the shoulder of Cynthia Whitson. 'Go ahead,' he told the wounded man. 'Talk.'

'If I got to die I want to tell you this an' get it off my chest. I didn't shoot that old man. I wanted Bragg to let him go. He kept us from gettin' the money all right, but hell; he had guts. I had no stomach for killin' him like that—in cold blood.'

They were all intently listening, even Carl Bragg, who growled at his pardner, 'Hank; you're *not* goin' to die. You lost a little blood but you're only drilled in the shoulder. Quit talkin'.'

Flint Manly turned on Bragg. 'Open

your mouth just one more time,' he said softly and intently, then left the threat uncompleted.

Gibson smiled at Cynthia. 'You been right kind, ma'am,' he said. 'Once I knew a lady like you. Funny what a man'll do with his life, ain't it?' Gibson closed his eyes and settled slightly. Fletcher removed his cigar, staring. Cynthia was stunned. Both the Broken Bow cowboys who'd been helping Gibson turned stiff and staring.

'Hell,' muttered one of them. 'He can't...A man don't just up'n die from a busted shoulder.'

Fletcher straightened up, stepped back and said, 'One of you throw that old blanket over him. Maybe a man can't die from a busted shoulder, but this one just did.' He turned and walked over where Flint Manly and Will Duran were standing looking incredulous.

Even Carl Bragg was nonplussed. Finally he said, 'I'll be damned.'

CHAPTER 14

Out in the alleyway behind the jail-house there was a sudden rush of booted feet, along with some rough words. Because it was so still and quiet out in the pre-dawn, those noises carried easily to the people inside the jailhouse. Then a terrific jolt back there jarred every timber and window inside. Fletcher clamped down hard on his cigar, stepped over to the cell-room door and flung it open. 'Come here,' he said to Carl Bragg. 'Move, man, *move!*'

Bragg moved, but slowly, so Flint Manly jumped over and gave him a savage shove. Bragg stumbled, glared over his shoulder and fetched up over where Fletcher bent to unlock a cell and swing back the door. Bragg walked inside just as another of those terrific jolts jarred the building. Fletcher locked the cell door, pocketed the key and jerked his head for the others to come with him. He drew his sixgun as he turned and limped swiftly down through the gloomy, stale-smelling little corridor that ran along in front of the cells to a storage space beyond the last cell. There, he pointed towards a little high, narrow window with steel bars in front of it. 'Get up there,' he ordered. 'Knock out the glass and fire off a few rounds then get down. They'll fire back.' As the others moved to obey, looking grim but mystified, Fletcher said, pointing to the steel-bound oaken back-alley door. 'They've got a battering ram.'

He was right. As someone dragged

over a bench for the others to stand up so they could see out the little barred window, another of those staggering blows hit the back-wall of the jail-house. The door didn't give but the log jambs on both sides of it groaned ominously. Howard Harrison smashed glass, poked his sixgun through and fired downward and slightly to his left. A man cried out. Flint Manly and Will Duran also poked their sixguns out and fired. It was too dark in the alley for accurate sighting, but the effect was instantaneous. The lynch-mob out there dropped their log and scattered to the four winds. Several angry shots were fired in the direction of the window but only one bullet came through and lodged itself spitefully in the overhead rafters.

Duran and Manly dropped down. Howard Harrison squeezed sideways alongside the broken window and continued to fire. He emptied his sixgun before he too stepped down off the bench. The return-shots were more numerous now, but they were even less accurate than the initial return-shots had been; evidently Harrison's stubborn gunfire had driven the lynchers even farther away.

Will Duran dropped his cigar, stepped on it and reached up with his gun-hand to mop sweat off his forehead, although this was the coolest time of day, the hour before sunrise. He said, looking straight at Fletcher, 'I don't believe it. It's crazy. Who'd follow him in what he's tryin' to do?'

From back up the hallway Carl Bragg heard that and called back in his gruff, blunt way. 'All you got to believe, feller, is that they got guns that shoot. That's all you got to worry about.'

It was true, of course, even though it wasn't altogether true. There was more to worry about, for as Fletcher said,

'If the town doesn't rally to us after sunrise, we're not in a very good spot, in here.'

Will was still stunned. 'But good Lord, Fletcher; there are some decent people in Evanston. They aren't all runnin' with that pack of wolves out there—are they?'

Fletcher didn't answer. He told Manly's two Broken Bow men to stay back there and keep a watch just in case those rammers returned and tried breaking in the back door again. He then took the others back out to the front office where Cynthia was standing over by the desk, her eyes round and very dark. Fletcher forced a smile and patted her shoulder. 'Not much to fret over,' he told her. 'Short of dynamite they can't get past these walls if we don't want them to.'

'But,' the girl murmured. 'How can this be happening, Sheriff?'

Fletcher didn't answer. He stepped

past, flattened alongside the wall near one of the two grilled front windows, and risked a look out into the paling, deserted roadway. Here and there he saw a light sputter to life up and down the roadway. Up towards the north end of town a man garrulously called out asking what was going on down there in the centre of town. He got no answer, or if he got one, Fletcher couldn't hear it.

Flint Manly was filling his pistol from his belt-loops over near the bench where Hank Gibson's blanket-shrouded body lay. Duran went across to the *olla* and deeply drank. They were worried, those two, and didn't try to hide it. Fletcher kept his vigil at the window, praying for full daylight to hasten along. He said, without turning towards the others, that he was confi-dent, once the town knew what was going on, it would turn against Munzer and his lynch-mob. Will Duran's answer to that was brusque.

'Yeah. If there's anyone left to turn against 'em. Seems to me he's got about half the town with him already.'

Fletcher turned. There was a small sheet-steel wood stove in the office, and a box of firewood. He said, 'Cynthia; how about stokin' up a fire an' making us all a cup of coffee; everything you'll need is on that shelf above the stove.' As the girl moved across the little room to obey she kept her eyes rigidly forward. She didn't glance at the blanket-shape on the bench even once.

Dawn came softly and silently. To Fletcher, it seemed ominous instead of gently refreshing as it usually seemed. He even heard a milk cow bawl and a rooster crow. Flint Manly came to ask where everyone was. Fletcher shook his head. He'd have liked to know that himself.

'They'll be planning something, no

doubt,' he said. 'And as long as we dasn't leave this building, Flint, I reckon we just wait.'

Manly turned as the coffee-aroma replaced the staleness of the jailhouse. Bragg called through from the back room. He'd also smelled that coffee.

Fletcher saw movement over across the road, up north in the direction of the *Claybank Bar & Restaurant*. He tried to pinpoint it and failed. As he was doing this Howard Harrison came up to him.

'Fletcher; I can sneak out of here,' he said. 'I've just been out back talking to those Broken Bow riders. They can give me enough cover to get clear.'

Fletcher turned a jaundiced eye. 'And after that,' he dryly asked, 'what? They'd hunt you down like a pack of terriers after a rat. Don't forget that's a lynch-mob out there, and you're the main one they want to lynch.'

'We can't stay holed up in here for ever.'

'I doubt if we'll have to,' said Fletcher, straightening around to look out his window once more. 'Forever is a long time.'

There *was* movement up by the *Claybank*, but as yet all the night-time shadows weren't dispelled because the town faced north and south, while the rising sun came up over in the east. That made shadows along the opposite side of the roadway from the jailhouse. It was the mingling of men and those shadows that impeded Fletcher's view of the northward road-way. But he was confident there were men up there doing something. What troubled him especially was what they were up to.

Flint Manly came up with two tin cups. He handed Fletcher one and said, 'Harrison's right, Fletcher. One of us has got to get out of here before they hit up again. If I go, I can get my men at the ranch and come back.'

Fletcher thanked Flint for the coffee, sipped it, made a face because it wasn't just bitter, it was also scalding hot, then he said, 'I'll go, Flint. You'd be forever getting out to Broken Bow and back. Harrison—well, he doesn't know the country, the town, or even the people. They'd catch him sure. Then Munzer'd string him up out there across the road right in front of our eyes. He's crazy enough to do just that.'

Manly sipped and looked around and lowered his voice. 'What could you do out there?' he asked.

Fletcher shrugged. 'There's a young husky feller who works at the livery-barn for Frank Cowdrey. Yesterday when he drove Miss Whitly up to the Whitson place he said something, Flint: He said he disliked Munzer as sheriff. Something to that effect. Then there's Miss Whitly too.'

'Fletcher,' said Manly tartly. 'She's the one that give those possemen out there free ammunition, remember?'

'That was before yesterday,' exclaimed Fletcher, sipping the acrid black coffee. 'I'll tell you one thing, Flint; if we don't get some help, we're goin' to all wind up lynched anyway, so one of us has got to make the effort. I'll try first. If they catch me you'll damned well hear it. Then someone else'll have to take a turn.'

Manly nodded, swished his coffee to cool it, and drank, looking sombrely over the edge of his cup at Fletcher Markley. 'Good luck,' he said, and lowered the cup. 'Come on; we'll go out back together like we're just havin' a look around. No sense in gettin' everyone all stirred up.'

That's exactly how the two older men left the office; as though they simply were strolling off on an inspection trip.

Manly's brace of riders were back there, one smoking, the other keeping watch by standing upon the little bench beneath the window. When Fletcher asked if they'd seen anything, the smoking man shook his head and the one beside the window said, 'There was a feller watchin' back there for a while, but I reckon he's gone now. At least he hasn't shown himself for the last fifteen minutes or such a matter.'

Fletcher went to the lock, inserted a brass key from his pocket and twisted. The lock was jammed, probably as a result of all that fierce ramming the night before. He swore, and worked the key back and forth while the others intently watched. Finally, Flint Manly walked over and heaved his weight against the door. This helped a little; the key turned a fraction farther. Flint called for his men to come over and help. When all three of them rammed the door from the inside, the key turned suddenly and easily, but the door-bracings were sprung, so when the lock gave, the door sprang part way open. Only the continuing pressure of those three cowmen kept it from flopping all the way open.

'Hold it,' said Fletcher, leaning his weight into the door also as he looked out into the alleyway where there was sufficient dawn-light to make visibility fairly good. He saw nothing extraordinary and he knew this alleyway as well as anyone; for a very long time he'd tied horses out there and had even used that alleyway door a time or two bringing in prisoners he didn't want lynched. He knew the shadows and the sheds, and he concluded that if there was a watcher out there, he'd have to be in one of the sheds because he was not otherwise visible.

He eased back. Flint raised an eyebrow at him. Fletcher palmed his sixgun, nodded at Flint and said, 'It looks safe enough. When I jump out there you slam this damned door and lock it.' He turned, took one more look out, then, balancing forward to rush out, he was detained by someone around front, across from the jail-house calling to him from among the stores over there.

Manly said, 'Go on; they want to palaver, which might mean they're all around front. Good luck, Fletcher.' That calling out front continued. Fletcher eased out, drew down a big breath and jumped as far forward as he could before he lit down running. Nothing happened. He got across the shadowy alleyway, in among some abandoned old wood- and cow-sheds over there, breathing hard, and flattened, waiting for the gunshot that never came. Out front that voice was still calling his name, only now it was angry and threatening. He turned left and right, satisfied himself it was safe to do so, and began passing back and forth on his way down to the livery-barn.

The place was deserted. Someone had put the horses he and Will and Flint and the others had used, reaching town the night before, into box-stalls, but that husky young hostler he'd hoped to find wasn't anywhere around. He went forward, eased around the roadway opening and looked up the roadway where that same angry, virulent voice was shouting across at the jailhouse.

He heard Flint Manly answer, and wondered how long it would take for Munzer, or whoever that was yelling towards the jailhouse, to realise Fletcher Markley wasn't answering.

A horse nickered behind him and pawed his stall partition. He apparently was thirsty or hungry, or maybe both. Fletcher turned. It was Manly's

Broken Bow animal. Fletcher straightened up as an idea came to him, then he went down there, led that Broken Bow horse out, checked up his reins so he couldn't get his head down, scribbled a hasty note with the stub of a pencil from one of his pockets, forced the note under the seating leather just aft of the saddle's gullet where it couldn't help but be found, then he led the horse out back and slapped him smartly over the rump with his hat. The horse snorted and jumped, then raced away out across the open country northwest of town with his head and tail up. He hadn't been either hungry or thirsty, he'd been bored and restless from being cooped up all night in that little twelve-by-twelve stall.

The yelling was still going on up the roadway. Fletcher could make out enough of it to realise that Munzer was offering to let the others inside the jailhouse go, if they'd hand over Howard Harrison and Carl Bragg. He went up to the doorway again, looking and listening. It sounded as though Munzer were in Whitly's general store. He wasn't certain of that at all, but his voice seemed to be coming from up there.

Fletcher could cross the roadway into the west-side alleyway without much difficulty; there were several big freight rigs parked along the plank-walk which would shield him as he went. Also, there was that dusty but elegant top-buggy which belonged to Angela Whitly parked out there too. He decided to try slipping around through the yonder alley, up north-ward if he could possibly make it, into the back of the general store. If he could just be lucky enough to nail Munzer and perhaps Frank Cowdrey, he was confident the other lynchers, without their leaders, would call the whole thing off.

He left the barn, passed down the far side of the first wagon, the second wagon, and got undetected down as far as Angela Whitly's top-buggy before he had to sprint fifty feet to the corner of the yonder buildings. He waited, peering closely up where the angry argument was still in progress, saw his chance and ran for it.

He made it.

CHAPTER 15

The reason he made it was someone up
the roadway fired a gun at the
jailhouse. The musical tinkle of
breaking glass meant the bullet had
struck one of the roadway windows,
and beyond any doubt, this act
intervened in Fletcher Markley's
favour. Everyone was concentrating
upon the scene of struggle up in the
centre of town.

As he flattened alongside a building
to catch his breath and plan what he
must do next, it occurred to him that
someone inside the jailhouse might
have been hit by that bullet. He

couldn't recall, in the brief moment he permitted himself to dwell upon it, ever before feeling so frustrated and betrayed in his entire lifetime.

He edged along his building to the entrance to the back alleyway, knelt and peeked around. There was no one in sight up there, but the sun was high enough to shine downward, making any secret progress northward up the alleyway highly susceptible to detection.

Someone spoke behind him in a quiet drawl. Fletcher whirled, swinging his gun to bear. It was the husky hostler from Frank Cowdrey's livery-barn. He'd evidently expected some such show of surprise, for he'd stepped in between the front of Angela Whitly's top-buggy and the wagon directly in front of it.

'Take it calm, Sheriff,' he said. 'This is Alf; the feller who works for Mister Cowdrey who drove that lady up to Whitson's place yesterday. I ain't gunnin' for you, so just tip down that pistol barrel a mite, will you?'

Fletcher lowered his weapon and waited for Alf to peer out, then to step out and amble on over towards him. As he walked along Alf looked up the roadway; as he did that he also kept talking. He said, 'Sheriff; if they discover you got out o' that jailhouse they'll be after you like a herd of bulls.' Alf came down alongside the building and gazed upon Fletcher where he still knelt. What struck Fletcher was that the liverybarn day-man wasn't the least bit upset or frightened. He grinned a little at Fletcher and jutted his chin towards the alleyway. 'You'll never make it, if you're fixin' to sneak along up there an' come in from behind 'em. Anyway; they're inside. I been watchin' from the barn loft. They're in all the stores on both sides of the jailhouse. When they open up they'll whittle them log walls down an inch at a time.'

Fletcher raised up gingerly to favour his game leg. He holstered his forty-five and said, 'How come you're not with 'em, Alf?'

The hostler shook his head. He was nearly as tall as Fletcher and was easily as heavy. He looked to be no more than perhaps Howard Harrison's age —in his mid-twenties somewhere. 'Well sir,' he drawled, leaning upon the building. 'Like I told you yesterday, Sheriff, I figure Cowdrey and Munzer an' that Jack Phipps or whatever his name is, along with them other simpletons like that Maddon feller, just don't have it. Don't have good sense an' don't have anythin' right on their side. I just hit this town three weeks back, but I've been in a lot of other towns just like it. There's always a herd of scatterbrains who think they're big enough to fit anyone's job. Them fellers up yonder are this town's crackpot fringe, as I see it.'

Fletcher nodded, sized up the hostler and said, 'Alf; I want to get into the building where Munzer and his friends are. Which one is it?'

'The gen'l store,' replied Alf matter-of-factly. 'Like I said, I been lyin' up there in the haymow watchin'. I saw Munzer and Cowdrey and a couple other fellers go into the gen'l store before they commenced all that yellin' back and forth.' Alf shook his head. 'But you'd never even get close, Sheriff. Too much sunlight now to use the alley, and you wouldn't last two minutes walkin' up the sidewalk for everyone to see.'

Fletcher didn't have the latter idea in mind, and now he didn't even consider going up the alley. He said, 'Alf; they won't shoot at you. How much guts have you got?'

Alf grinned. 'Enough, Sheriff. Try me.'

'Go up there through the alleyway; tell Munzer I'm down in the liverybarn saddling a horse, then get out of the way.'

Alf's smile dwindled. He gazed long and hard at Fletcher. 'You plumb sure this is how you want it?' he eventually asked. 'Sheriff; Munzer won't come alone.'

Fletcher said, 'No, Alf, and I won't be in the liverybarn either. Now go on.'

Alf straightened up off the building, pursed his lips in thought, then stepped around Fletcher and went ambling along into the alleyway. He didn't wear a gun; at least he didn't have one showing.

Fletcher's conscience pricked him. He was sending the youthful livery-barn day-man squarely into trouble.

Alf owed Evanston and Fletcher Markley nothing; he'd only been in the town three weeks. Fletcher moved away, heading towards those oak-walled freight wagons again, justifying what he'd done on the grounds of necessity.

Up the road several shots were fired into the jailhouse again, but this time an answering volley came back, breaking windows, smashing wooden siding, and causing someone up there on Munzer's side of the road to let off a howl of fright.

Fletcher paused beside a wagon to listen. Evidently Flint and the others inside the jailhouse were out of patience. They followed up that initial volley with another one just as thunderous and evidently just as devastating, from the sounds of smashed boards and breaking windows up the road. He grinned to himself, started up the side of the wagon and dropped down inside it. The freight outfit had last been used to haul loose grain of some kind, oats or barley evidently, because grains of the stuff were thickly underfoot as Fletcher stooped to look around.

Like all freight wagons used on the desert, this one had five-foot-high rear wheels with tyres of steel six inches across. This precluded the dangers of a weighted rig becoming stuck fast in the summertime sand. The sidewalls were six-feet-high and made of planed oak. They would turn a bullet, an arrow, or withstand the pressure of a load of something as bulky and heavy as loose grain.

Fletcher checked his sixgun and waited. He had no doubt that Munzer would come. Neither did he doubt but that Munzer wouldn't be alone. He'd planned on that; he'd never, right from the beginning of all this trouble, had any desire to shoot it out with

Munzer or Cowdrey or Phipps, or any of the other younger men who were being led along and influenced by Munzer and Cowdrey, but that firing upon the jailhouse, endangering Cynthia and all the other decent people in there, changed his mind. He meant now to shoot down the leaders of that wolf-pack out there if he could. He hoped he'd be able to accomplish it quickly enough to destroy the mob's leadership before the mob itself turned on him.

It was, he told himself, a wildly unlikely scheme, but he didn't have any decent alternatives. He'd waited as long as he dared for the decent element of Evanston to come out into the roadway with guns. Thus far that hadn't happened. Perhaps the decent people were waiting for something; for a leader perhaps or for some favourable event. Well; with any luck, Fletcher meant to provide them with both.

He heard men's voices coming around from the westerly alley. He tried to pick out the recognisable ones and failed because there were too many, all excited, all seemingly eager to catch him in the liverybarn. He dropped to one knee with his sixgun in hand, listening as that rushing crowd of armed men swept on across from the alleyway towards the wagon where he was hiding. He heard several slurred voices, several banal ones as well, and up to then he'd had no idea the lynchers had been drinking. Now, as he listened, waited and reflected, he thought he understood what they'd been doing up there in front of Will Duran's saloon just at daybreak. Drinking. Getting their courage up and plundering Duran's place as a peevish way of getting even with him for siding with Fletcher Markley.

Several men strode right past his hiding place growling threats and urging their companions to hasten, saying that if Markley was still in the barn they'd have to shoot him on sight because he was tough.

There was no way to peek out without raising up and being seen, so Fletcher had to wait until the last one of those hastening men rushed past, heading on towards the front of the liverybarn. Then, holding his breath, he slowly unwound. He had to look both ways because he had no way of telling whether more men were coming across the road from the west alley. He looked backwards first. There was one man back there. He was leaning against the wall of the building with a carbine held low in front of his body in both hands. He looked surprisingly cool and relaxed. It was the youth called Alf.

Fletcher looked ahead, raising his sixgun as he did so. Munzer was not in sight. He'd evidently already entered the barn. But the telegrapher was there. He happened to look up as Fletcher swung forward. He saw Fletcher; his jaw sagged, his eyes bulged, he nearly dropped the shotgun in his hands. He forced himself to bleat out a warning, then threw up the scattergun. Fletcher fired. Jack Phipps went backwards with both barrels of his scattergun pointing straight up when he yanked both triggers simultaneously. The resulting blow, plus the impact from Fletcher's bullet, knocked Phipps ten feet before he fell.

That deafening blast in the very doorway of the barn caused consternation. Men yelped and jumped every which way. Frank Cowdrey spun around, less distracted, to see what Phipps had been trying to shoot at. Fletcher called out to Cowdrey.

'Here, Frank!'

Cowdrey had his chance. He shot and jumped away and shot again, fell across Phipps's body and sprawled at exactly the second Fletcher fired at him. The bullet tore the crown out of Cowdrey's hat. Pandemonium broke. Guns exploded and terrified livery horses squealed and struck, adding to the bedlam. There were at least seven men in the barn, but only two or three of them had any idea what was happening. Frank Cowdrey, who owned the liverybarn, knew, but when his hat had been violently jerked off, Cowdrey, already floundering across the body of the telegrapher, lost control. He yelled and hurled himself away, dropped his sixgun and tried to frantically roll towards some kind of shelter.

Fletcher aimed low, held steady, then fired. Cowdrey cried out, his left leg broke over at an unnatural angle, and he rolled into a ball screaming with pain.

Several of those lynchers in the barn

runway stampeded. Fletcher could have nailed them one at a time as they fled wildly down through the barn, out the back-alley exit, and raced blindly to get away to the left and to the right.

A drunken man stepped out into the doorway, raised his rifle, and a bullet took him squarely in the centre of the forehead. He didn't even get to fire. Fletcher turned; Alf was just lowering his carbine. He was still standing across the road in plain sight, coolly watching.

Buster Munzer's voice yelled at the men to stand steady, but by the time Munzer could say this, and be heard over the screams and gunshots, he was almost alone in the barn, except for Frank Cowdrey, moaning and rocking back and forth as he held his broken leg, the telegrapher, who hadn't moved since Fletcher's gun had downed him, and that dead man Alf had picked off from across the road.

Fletcher dropped down inside his freight wagon, worked swiftly at reloading, then raised up gingerly again. The silence came, briefly, only to be broken by another shouted command from Buster Munzer. No one answered him. Fletcher tried to see down the runway better, couldn't, so he vaulted out of his wagon, lit on his left leg automatically, eased his weight onto the other leg, the game one, and started walking forward, sixgun up and cocked.

'No use, Sheriff,' called Alf, standing up straight back there. 'I just seen him run out the back way.'

'Who?' said Fletcher.

'Munzer, Sheriff. I just seen him run out like the rest of 'em did.' Alf started ambling on over. Fletcher waited until he was close, then told him to cover his back while he entered the barn. Alf nodded and took his casual stance.

Fletcher walked inside lightly, care-

268

fully. The barn smelled powerfully of burnt gunpowder. The terrified horses were still softly snorting, rolling their eyes or quivering in their stalls, but except for the dead and injured, Fletcher saw nothing to train his weapon upon.

He stepped over that drunk rifleman Alf had downed. He vaguely recognised the man as someone who'd been hanging around the saloons in town the past four or five weeks. A drifter; every summer Evanston got its share of them. Frank Cowdrey, face bathed in sweat, rolled over and looked straight up into Fletcher Markley's cocked sixgun. He froze; even the grimace of agony across his features froze. He whispered, 'Don't, Fletcher. Don't shoot. You busted my leg. I quit. I give up. Please—don't shoot.'

Fletcher looked around, still saw no one, and reached down to yank

Cowdrey up onto his good leg. 'Alf,' he called. 'Come in here and give your boss a hand.' Alf came, ambling along as casually as he always seemed to move.

Fletcher went to where Jack Phipps was lying. He knew what he'd find because Fletcher Markley rarely missed when he fired. He toed Phipps over onto his back. The bullet had taken him high, six or eight inches above the heart but dead centre. Phipps was dead. Fletcher picked up the shotgun Phipps had been carrying, broke it, ejected its pair of spent shells, rummaged through the dead man's jacket for a pair of re-loads, snapped the weapon closed and holstered his sixgun. He was now prepared for any kind of close-order combat anyone wished to offer.

Alf said, 'Sheriff; this here leg is busted pretty bad. Maybe I'd better take him up to the doctor's place on the north edge of town.'

'Like hell,' growled Fletcher, turning and gesturing with the shotgun. 'Walk him straight up the road to the jailhouse. Let's go. Anyone shoots at you or me—I shoot Cowdrey. Walk out!'

CHAPTER 16

Undoubtedly the disaster at the livery-barn accounted for part of the fact that no one tried a killing shot at Fletcher Markley, the ex-sheriff, as he prodded the wounded man and his helper on up the roadway out in sight of anyone wishing to look. But then too, Fletcher Markley walked on the inside, next to the buildings, so close to Frank Cowdrey and with his shotgun pushed into Cowdrey's back so obviously, that if there was a would-be assassin around, he didn't try it. If he had, he'd probably have missed Fletcher and struck Cowdrey, or the liverybarn hostler.

When they reached the jailhouse the door swung inward and Flint Manly was standing back with a carbine levelled and cocked, not at Fletcher and his companions, but at anyone beyond them over across the roadway, who might choose this particular moment to renew the gunfight. No one did. Markley stood aside for Alf and Frank Cowdrey to enter, then pushed the door closed and barred it from the inside.

'Cynthia,' he said, looking around for the girl. 'Here's another one for you to patch up. I reckon this one'll make it all right—if I don't slit his throat just on general principles.'

Manly motioned for his two range-riders to lend Cowdrey a hand. The cowboys came forward, took Cowdrey over to the same bench where the defunct outlaw, Hank Gibson, was cooling out, and held Cowdrey there.

One of them said in a dry drawl, 'Say, Mack; you reckon that feller's stiff enough yet to prop in a corner while we use this here bench to carve up another one?' The cowboy called Mack stooped, lifted the blanket from the dead man's grey features, made certain Frank Cowdrey got a good look, then said, 'Nope; I figure it'll take him another hour to get that stiff. But I'll tell you what we can do—just ease him over a mite an' lay this one right down nice and comfy beside him.'

Cowdrey twisted in the grip of those two cowboys, shot Fletcher a frantic look and said, 'Get me away from these two. Listen; I'm bleedin' bad, Fletcher. I got to have help.'

'Broken leg,' muttered Flint Manly, and shook his head. 'Reckon we'll have to shoot him.' He reached for his sixgun and Cowdrey, already over-wrought and badly injured, dropped down in the arms of those two Broken Bow men, in a dead faint.

The cowboys were amazed. They dragged him to a corner, eased him down and wagged their heads as Cynthia came over to kneel and examine the leg. The one named Mack said, 'Ma'am; there must be some kind o' a bad curse in this place. Every time we get hold of a wounded feller, he dies. Now who ever seen a man faint dead away like that just from a busted leg?'

From across the road a rifle slammed a large-calibre slug into the jailhouse. Everyone flinched. Howard Harrison said that wasn't any Winchester carbine. Will Duran, in the act of lighting a cigarette, dropped the match and dropped right down on top of it. That rifleman let go with another bullet. This one came through one of the smashed roadside windows and cracked a floor planking less than a foot from where Flint Manly was standing.

Manly jumped like he'd been stung, ran over and flattened up against the front wall.

'That,' he pronounced, 'isn't a carbine. That's a damned big-game rifle. Look at the hole it made in the floor.'

No one argued with Manly's pronouncement. Everyone got away from the two front windows except Cynthia. She was making a cloth tourniquet for Frank Cowdrey's broken leg.

Fletcher went across to her, knelt and took hold of Frank Cowdrey, straightened up with the unconscious man across one shoulder and went over in front of the roadway door. There, with Cynthia helping, he put the wounded man back down.

Cynthia said, 'Thank you, Sheriff,' and Fletcher smiled at her, stepped away and eased up to the other front window. The third shot from that big-bore rifle slammed into the front of the jailhouse. Everyone standing over there could feel the impact. Duran said, 'He won't hit any of us, but if he's figurin' on demoralising us, he's sure succeeding with me.'

Fletcher looked around. Duran was flat out on the floor twenty feet back across the room. Fletcher said, 'Will; can you see out my window?' Duran could and nodded his head that this was so. 'Then where's the firing from?' asked Fletcher.

'From atop the general store,' replied Duran, and ducked as the next one of those big slugs came through the window and ploughed out a big wood splinter from the floor. Duran rolled like a log to get over against the front wall with the others. Not until he'd bumped the legs of Howard Harrison did he even attempt to arise. Then he did, clutching a Winchester saddle-gun and looking anxious. 'That kind of gunfire scares hell out of me,' he told the younger man. 'One time, when I was a boy, I saw a man shot accidentally by a buffalo rifle.' Duran rolled his eyes in horror, indicating that what he'd seen had been horrifying.

The others, while showing less actual fear, were nevertheless full of respect for that sniper atop the store building. One of the Broken Bow men, standing in the open back-room doorway, hunkered down a little so he'd be able to see out Flint Manly's front window, and the next one of those big lead slugs tore out a large chunk of wood where his head had been moments before. The cowboy dropped like lead and rolled back out of sight into the cell-room. This caused Carl Bragg to laugh. The cowboy jumped up and lunged, but Bragg was just as quick; he got away from the front of his cell.

Manly turned and said, 'Fletcher; can you see him?'

Fletcher said he couldn't see the sniper yet, but he also said, 'Flint; I think from the way he's firing that thing, it's got to be a single-shot rifle. He shoots it, then has to lie low while he ejects, then re-loads. Wait until he lets go with the next one, then we'll both step out and try a shot at him.'

Manly nodded, raised his carbine and waited. No one moved throughout the room until Frank Cowdrey groaned. Then all but Flint Manly and Fletcher Markley turned to look down. At the same moment the rifleman over across the road fired. At once Manly and Markley stepped ahead, pushed out their carbines and hesitated a second or two seeking a target, then Fletcher fired. He'd seen the smallest tip of a hat on the yonder roof; he'd drawn down as far as he dared before he fired. The bullet struck wood, splintered a length of siding, and ploughed on through. Manly, using Fletcher's sighting, also fired. They then both levered and fired again. There was no way of telling whether they'd hit the sniper or not, but when they both eased back from their windows to wait for the next enemy shot, none was fired back at them.

Flint wiped his face and blew out a big breath. He turned, shook his head over at Fletcher, and got back a wry grin.

Silence settled now, and for almost ten minutes it lingered before someone out back of the jailhouse called to those inside. At once the pair of Broken Bow rangeriders disappeared down the little corridor towards the back of the building. Simultaneously, out front, a crashing volley of gunfire erupted all up and down the yonder roadway. Bullets sped through both the roadway windows and splattered back and forth upon the outer wall. Howard Harrison and Will Duran poked carbines out and blindly returned that fire. Fletcher was reloading when one of the cowboys appeared over in the cell-room doorway.

'Hey, Sheriff,' he sang out over the crash and rattle of guns. 'There's a feller out back says help's on the way. He says he seen a bunch of riders comin' from the direction of Broken Bow.'

The liverybarn hostler, Alf, walked over, picked up a carbine off the sheriff's desk, stepped to the window, exposed himself for a moment, and fired once, then jumped back. Across the road a man fell head-first out of a smashed window and hung there until his dying kicks and jerks let him drop down onto the plankwalk. Fletcher looked at Alf, then at the Broken Bow cowboy, and walked over towards the latter. When he was almost through the cell-room door he turned and said, 'Alf; come with me. Bring along that carbine.'

He took the husky, younger man down to the back door with him, where the second cowboy was standing, then motioned for the men to help him open the sprung door again. One of the cowboys protested. 'Sheriff; you can't go out there again. Man; they'll get you sure this time. Anyway, if there's help comin', what's the sense of it?'

'Because,' said Fletcher, 'I want to see for myself that help *is* coming. If it is, then I want to get around this town and cut off the escape of those men who've been attacking us.' He gestured. 'Now lean on that door when I insert the key. Alf; you're a pretty good shot; you come along with me.'

The Broken Bow men ambled up to the door looking morose. Cynthia came down the corridor, diverting all of them. She said, 'Sheriff; there are some people up at the north end of town who want to talk.'

Fletcher turned, frowning. 'What people?' he asked. 'What do they want to talk about?'

Cynthia shook her head, turned and motioned towards the doorway leading back into the office. 'I don't know. I was bandaging Mister Cowdrey's leg when someone threw a stone inside from over across the road. There's a note. Mister Manly thinks you'd better come see for yourself.'

Fletcher hesitated, looking at the men with him and at the steel-bound door. He said, 'I'll be back in a minute,' and went along behind Cynthia back into the office.

Flint Manly had both the stone and the note which had been tied to it. He handed them to Fletcher without a word. Over along the front wall stood the others, waiting and watching. Outside the embattled building the morning sunshine pleasantly shined, but with an accumulating heat. It was quiet out there and except for the fact that the roadway was absolutely deserted at the time of day when it was usually quite busy, it seemed drowsily normal.

Manly pointed to the northerly front window where he'd been standing for some time, and said, 'I didn't see that rock coming until about twenty feet before it sailed through my window, then the sunlight struck that white paper and I ducked. Whoever flung the thing was over across the road, maybe between a couple of buildings, I didn't see him. But I'll tell you one thing for a fact, he was using a slingshot when he let go with that stone. Otherwise it wouldn't have been comin' so fast when it clipped through the window.'

Fletcher read the note. All it said was that a committee of citizens was in one of the northerly houses up the road and wanted to talk to Fletcher Markley; that if Fletcher would fling the rock out into the back-alley, they'd be watching, and would come at once to the back door of the jailhouse. That was all; there was no signature.

Flint scratched his head, waiting for Fletcher to say something. When Fletcher stood there looking at the note, Manly finally said, 'I figure it for a trick.'

Fletcher raised his eyes. 'Maybe. But they wouldn't dare sign that note anyway. If Munzer's crew got hold of it there'd be another execution out there.' He turned. Over in the doorway Alf was idly leaning upon his borrowed carbine. Frank Cowdrey groaned and weakly rolled his head back and forth where he lay upon the floor, whispering for water. Howard

Harrison went to get him some.

Fletcher said, 'Flint; you keep a close watch out there in front. If it is a trick, you can expect 'em to hit us hard out there when they figure we're all in the back room.' He turned, went over where Alf eased back for Fletcher to pass through, then he jerked his head at the younger man.

Those two Broken Bow cowboys were smoking and slouching against the steel-bound rear door. Fletcher handed one of them the rock. 'Get up onto that bench,' he said, 'and toss that thing out into the alleyway. Not hard now, mind you; just toss it out. As soon as you see someone out there, keep an eye on him while the rest of us get this door open. He's supposed to be a friend.'

The cowboys widened their eyes at Fletcher. One of them said dryly, 'A friend, Sheriff? Damned if I wasn't beginnin' to think we'd run out of friends.'

'If there's more than one of them let me know. We're only going to admit one man.'

The farthest cowboy stepped up onto the bench. His pardner and husky Alf leaned their considerable weight upon the sprung door while Fletcher inserted the key, looked up to see the cowboy on the bench toss out the little rock, then he also settled his shoulder against the panel and twisted. The key worked perfectly.

'See anyone?' Fletcher asked.

The watching rangerider said, 'Yeah. One feller slippin' down from the north wrapped in a buffler coat. Sheriff; it's too blessed hot out there for a man to be wearin' a buffler coat. This is beginnin' to smell like some kind of a trick, to me.'

Fletcher said, 'Just one?'

'Yeah, just this one feller in the buffler coat.'

'We'll take a chance on it being a

trick,' exclaimed Fletcher, easing off with his weight so the door coud swing inward slightly. 'Are there any more coming?'

'Nope. Just Mister Buffler-coat, an' while he's likely got a pistol under his darned coat, he's sure got no rifle nor carbine. Swing it open a mite more, Sheriff. Here he comes.'

Fletcher nodded at his companions; all three of them slackened off still more, the door creaked and groaned, came open far enough to admit a person, and the stranger whisked through. Fletcher said, 'Close it,' and heaved his heft against the door. They got it closed and locked, then all of them stood there, dumbfounded. The buffalo coat was dropped to the floor, the intruder tossed down the hat too, and it wasn't a man at all, it was Angela Whitly!

Fletcher, just as astonished as the others, stood for a moment just staring. Up the corridor Flint Manly who was standing beside Howard Harrison up there, both with carbines up and ready, said, 'Well I'll be double damned,' and lowered his weapon.

Fletcher looked around. The cowboy on the bench was staring with his mouth open at Angela Whitly. Fletcher growled at him. 'Any more out there?' The cowboy looked, then shook his head.

Angela said, 'It isn't a trick, Sheriff Markley. I came alone.'

'Why the coat?' he asked.

She smiled at him. Without it, there could never have been any question in anyone's mind that she was a woman, not a man. 'It seemed advisable,' she murmured, and did not elaborate. Then she said, turning brisk and business-like, 'Sheriff; there are ten armed men up at the doctor's house on the north edge of town. More are coming. We had to get word to you that we intend to get around behind Mister Munzer and his men, and attack them. Otherwise, we were afraid that in the fighting you and your friends in here would mistake us for more enemies.'

Fletcher gazed straight at the handsome woman. 'We?' he said. She nodded, repeating the word. Then she said she'd had no idea how awfully wrong she'd been before, when she'd supported Munzer against Fletcher Markley, but that now she meant to rectify that.

'You mean,' said one of the cowboys, 'You're goin' to fight too—with a gun—ma'am?'

Angela nodded. 'Something I learned a long time ago when I was a little girl, cowboy, is that a rifle fits any kind of shoulder—male or female. Besides, those people up there are uncertain; they have no leader. The only thing we're all agreed upon is that what Mister Munzer and his friends are doing is terribly wrong. We aren't going to stand by any longer and let him do it.'

Fletcher began shaking his head and darkly scowling even before Angela Whitly was finished. 'You're not goin' to leave this jailhouse if you mean to actively fight,' he told her, then raised his head and called down the corridor: 'Flint; Alf; come here.'

CHAPTER 17

Angela started to protest. Fletcher ignored that and said, 'Flint; this boy here is cool under fire and he's good with a gun. You can take your choice; either go back up there with Miss Whitly and lead those townsmen, or stay here and keep Munzer out of this jailhouse.'

One of the Broken Bow cowboys said, 'Sheriff; I got a question.' Evidently it had just struck this man that what had occurred might be a trick. 'Who was that feller who called over to us just before this here lady come along, that help was on the way?'

Fletcher looked from the rangeman to Angela. She said, 'He was the man sent over here by Munzer to see that none of you tried escaping by the back door.'

'Then how—?'

'He is one of us,' explained Angela. 'Munzer thinks he's one of his friends, but he isn't that at all. Otherwise, I'd never have been able to get down here.'

Fletcher conceded that with a short statement. 'She's plumb right about one thing; if she'd been seen slippin' down the alley by one of Munzer's sentries, he'd have probably shot her.'

'All right,' admitted the cowboy, clinging stubbornly to his suspicions. 'But all that means is that she could also be on Munzer's side, Sheriff.'

Markley grimly smiled. 'I'm not overlooking that,' he said, and looked straight at Angela Whitly as he spoke. 'But it's a risk we're goin' to have to run because we sure need help.' He paused, swinging his attention to Flint and Alf. 'Well?' he said to the older man.

Manly shrugged. 'Either way you want it, Fletcher. I'd just as soon go up there with her, or if you like I'll stay here an' mind the fort, an' you can go.'

Fletcher balanced that decision on the edge of his mind briefly before stepping back to scoop up the shotgun he'd laid aside to open the door for Angela Whitly. He said, 'Alf; you come with me. Flint; for gosh sakes keep 'em out or they'll not only lynch Bragg and Howard Harrison—they'll cut down every man and woman in here with you.' He turned towards the door, remembered something, and turned back. 'By the way,' he said to Manly, 'I checked up your horse, stuck a note under the seat-leather and sent him out to Broken Bow an hour or more ago. By now, if he got there and if they found that note, your riders ought to be heading for town armed and loaded for lions.' He then turned back, motioned for the others to heave their combined weight against the sprung door again, and fished out his key. 'Get ready, Miss Whitly,' he said, inserted the key, rolled his shoulder against the panel and twisted. The key worked, the door jumped inward, and a rush of hot morning sunlight came inside. 'Alf; go ahead of Miss Whitly.' As he gave that order, Fletcher stepped back, nodded, then tossed the door key to Flint. 'Lock it after us.'

They were outside moving swiftly when Alf suddenly swung his carbine. Angela called sharply. 'No!' Alf hesitated and the armed man standing between two buildings watching that upraised carbine, slumped at the shoulders. He'd been badly shaken by his near call. As he walked forward he kept eyeing Alf. Then he put that interlude out of his mind and said, 'Miz Whitly; the others are gettin' impatient.'

Fletcher recognised the man; he worked in the freight yard for Buster Munzer, and also occasionally at the liverybarn which was owned in some kind of loose partnership between Munzer and Cowdrey. To test him Fletcher said, 'What's Buster up to, over across the road?'

The man answered promptly. 'He's takin' a page from your book, Sheriff; him and four or five of his friends are down there riggin' out a freight wagon they figure to drive right up in front of the jailhouse where they can keep everyone away from the windows while they shoot down the door.'

This startling piece of information stopped Fletcher in his tracks. For a moment he hung there about half willing to turn back to warn the others.

Angela Whitly must've seen this in his face, for she said, speaking to the sentry, 'Go back and get that information to the men in the jailhouse. Then, if they need you, help them.'

The sentry nodded, muttered, 'Yes'm,' and stalked off.

Angela led them from this point on. They got to the doctor's house, were admitted through the rear door, and were surrounded by armed men with anxious, troubled faces, when a furious volley of gunfire erupted down the yonder roadway.

Fletcher shouldered through, ignoring the questions fired at him, nodded brusquely at the physician whose house he was in, and reached the front door where he peered out expecting to see that oak-sided freight wagon out front of the jailhouse. What he actually saw was something altogether different. There was a fight around one of the freight rigs all right, but it was still parked down near the livery-barn, and the men inside it were firing and yelling at a string of hard-riding cowboys sweeping in from the southwest, guns blazing and raising the Texas Yell.

Alf was beside Fletcher but Markley didn't realise it until the younger man said, 'Well; it took 'em long enough. That'll be Mister Manly's Broken Bow riders, won't it, Sheriff?'

Fletcher nodded, scowling. 'The damned fools; charging in like that could get half of 'em cut down before they even get close.'

But even as Fletcher said that, the oncoming riders split off left and right, careening along in a reckless zig-zag riding pattern which made them practically impossible to hit. They poured a fierce volley of gunfire into that freight rig down where Munzer and his friends were, then swept up the side of town on the east and west, their gunfire diminishing as targets became scarcer.

One of the armed townsmen peering out breathed a big sigh and said, 'That ought to show Munzer he isn't goin' to bulldoze this town!'

Fletcher stepped back, closed the door and looked at the men. Even the physician had a carbine in his fist and a pistol belted to his rather ample middle. Fletcher shook his head at him. 'Doc; you stay inside. You'll have your share after the fighting's over. And keep this lady in here with you. The rest of you men got enough guns and ammunition?' They held up their weapons, crowding in close to hear every word, because the gunfire was raggedly brisking up again, down at the south end of town where, evidently, those Broken Bow riders had dismounted on the fly and had run in between buildings to engage the men around the freight wagons again.

'Now listen close,' Fletcher exclaimed. 'We're going out of here in a rush. There's no other way to get across the road without taking an hour to filter across one at a time. They'll see you for sure, and they'll fire on us too, but don't stop. Keep running and never mind returning their fire. A stationary target out there in the middle of the road with plenty of sunlight all around, is an invitation to get killed. Remember what I'm telling you—run and don't stop running until you're in among the buildings over across the road. Rally over there and wait. I'm not the fastest runner you ever saw, so wait for me. You got that?'

They had. Even the physician was vigorously nodding his head. And Angela, who'd come up with a Winchester in her hands. Fletcher put a stiff glance upon those two. 'You stay. The both of you stay. Don't argue, ma'am. We don't have the time for it.' He hesitated, licked his lips, gave his Longhorn moustache a hard twist, then said, 'Maybe, after this is all over an' done with, we can discuss things over supper, but right now's not the time.'

Several of the men chuckled. Not all of them though, because these were not professional gunfighters, they were merchants and labourers and barkeepers, and they were also afraid. Resolute but afraid.

Fletcher searched out Alf in that crowd, beckoned him on up and said, 'In case this game leg of mine slows me down enough for one of them to nail me, you take over. Lead them down where the bunch of you can join up with Broken Bow. Then close in on those damned wagons and don't let up on the firing until there are no shots coming back. All right, Alf?'

The husky younger man nodded. 'All right, Sheriff,' he agreed. 'But you'll make it just fine.'

Fletcher turned to open the door. Angela Whitly pushed through and lightly lay a hand upon his straining big arm. When he opened the door and looked down, she said, 'Sheriff; would tomorrow night be too early for that supper?' She was smiling. It seemed to loosen all those men. They smiled too, watching Fletcher's bleak, forbidding countenance. He looked down at her a moment then the outer corners of his mouth lifted a little.

'No ma'am, tomorrow'd be just fine.' His eyes twinkled their appreciation for what she'd just done—easing the tension and the strangling fear. He flung open the door, stepped through and started dead ahead for the roadway.

Southward that sporadic gunfire was still going on. Several townsmen went past Fletcher Markley as though they'd been shot from cannons; they were doing exactly what he'd instructed them to do. They were running hard without looking right or left. As they whipped past, he had a feeling, from seeing their faces, that it probably wasn't altogether his instructions which spurred them on, for every time a gun rattled and crashed southward, they'd pick up another notch or two of speed.

For Fletcher it was slower going. He had that game leg. But aside from that he was a large, heavy man; running on foot just wasn't his strong suit.

Alf trotted up, looked right and left. They were the last two out there in the roadway. Southward a man's rising shout indicated some of Munzer's men had spotted them. Alf said, 'Sheriff; we're goin' to be shot at.' He said it so matter-of-factly that Fletcher grinned just before he sprang up onto the yonder plankwalk, slowed to catch his breath, and saw Alf lunge over to the edge of an upright post, raise his carbine and fire. Evidently Alf had spotted a target. Two seconds later a flash and roar of those guns down by the freight wagons showed that Munzer and his men weren't averse to this brief diversion. Bullets struck all around, in wood, upon the plankwalk underfoot, into glass windows. Two of them even left neat round holes in the southward sign hanging above Will Duran's saloon.

Fletcher led them on through and out into the back alley. They were all breathing hard although the race hadn't been either distant nor prolonged. One of the men, older and grey and slightly more grizzled and checked than the others, dryly said, 'This is what Doc'd call high blood pressure, isn't it, Sheriff?'

Fletcher didn't know. He took them

down the alley until he spotted two men spreading out and turning towards them, carbines in hand, then he began calling out.

'Broken Bow! Hey Broken Bow! This is Fletcher Markley. If you want more guns, sing out, we're down here to lend a hand.'

One of those cowboys sang out, but what he said was unprintable. The other one raised up from around the corner of an old outhouse and wig-wagged with his hat. 'Down yere,' he called to Fletcher in an unmistakable Texas drawl. 'Right down yere, boys, an' we got front-row seats for anyone needin' to tie a knot in a lion's tail. Come along, Sheriff; we can use a mite of he'p. Fer townsmen them fellers around them yonder wagons got grit in their craws.'

Fletcher led his men straight down the alleyway, making no attempt to reach concealment. Broken Bow riders poked out a head here and there, peered from between buildings, or raised up waving their firearms recklessly, calling out droll comments. They were typical rangemen; tough and amiable, capable and deadly and fun-loving, all in the same breath.

Fletcher went all the way down to the far end of the alleyway, where it turned, which happened to also be the place where he'd earlier crouched, considering passing up this same alleyway. He knew those wagons were just around that corner, down there. He also knew that if he couldn't prevent it, when all the guns opened up, Munzer would probably try to withdraw into the liverybarn.

'Alf,' he called, and pointed overhead. 'See if you can get atop that building. Take a man or two with you if you'd like.'

Alf looked up, looked at Fletcher, then gently smiled. 'We'll pick 'em off like a bunch of grouse on a roostin' limb,' he drawled, turned, beckoned to a pair of men about his own age, and started back along the wall of the building, looking for a rear door.

Fletcher put his carbine against that same wall. Several of the townsmen were mystified; they thought Fletcher would start the fight right off. He turned, holding up his arms for all the firing to cease. It did, but only very gradually and evidently also very reluctantly.

'Buster,' he sang out, his deep-down voice rolling into the void left by the silenced guns. 'Buster, this is Fletcher Markley. You saw me run across the road up at the north end of town with some armed men. Well—you listen good now because I'm only goin' to say this once: Put down your weapons over there, get out of those wagons, and walk out into the centre of the road. Fetch along your men.'

Fletcher's words died out slowly, their echoes bouncing back and forth up the roadway. Then an answer came back. 'Markley; I'm not quitting until I get you. You've broken the law. You're outside the law and every damned man with you is the same! I'm sheriff here, an' I call on those men with you to disarm you and deliver you to me.'

'Buster,' said Fletcher. 'Get hold of yourself. You've turned Evanston into a battleground. You're trying to lynch two men. You're out of your mind if you think the law ever sanctions anything like what you're doing. Out of your mind, Buster!'

That repeated statement must have triggered Munzer's rage, because he began firing again, blindly, rapidly, and murderously. He screamed for the men with him to fire also. They did. Fletcher looked around. The men with him nodded soberly. He'd done his best. Now, guns would have to decide this issue.

CHAPTER 18

Something happened as Fletcher's men glided into positions up and down the westerly roadway where they began firing. Overhead, three carbines sniped and down there by the wagons a man cried out and tumbled down across the tongue and double-trees, the first casualty.

Munzer, seeing he couldn't possibly remain among the protective wagons as long as he was vulnerable from that overhead perch, cried out for his men to withdraw into the liverybarn, while at the same time pinning down those snipers up there.

That was when it happened: A loose rattle of gunfire from mid-way uptown, to out back of the liverybarn. Fletcher saw those flashes and heard the guns too. It wasn't Broken Bow because he had Manly's riders with him. He doubted that it could be more townsmen or cowmen, although that was certainly not impossible. Then he heard a cowboy yell and knew who it was: Flint and Will, Howard Harrison and the others from the jailhouse; They'd gone out the back way, evidently, having surmised that Munzer must retreat into the liverybarn, and were hastening down there now to prevent that from happening.

One of the townsmen came over, wiped his nose on the back of a soiled sleeve, and said, 'Sheriff; them fellers with Buster ain't goin' no place.'

Fletcher agreed and sent the man back to his firing position. He then tried yelling to Munzer one more time.

It was wasted effort; there was so much gunfire by now it was doubtful if anyone could even have heard a bugle blown—if there'd been such a thing, which there wasn't.

Fletcher removed his hat, lay belly-down and eased his face around the corner of his building to look out. Men were faintly visible through the cloud of dirty gunsmoke around the freight wagons. Even as he watched he saw the yellow flash of flame. He also saw pale marks where lead struck those oaken sideboards out there. Munzer was withdrawing rearward towards the liverybarn even though he must certainly have known he was flanked.

Overhead, a carbine would roar now and again. There was nothing frenetic or excited about this overhead gunfire. It seemed to Fletcher that Alf had instilled some of his dead calm into the men up there with him. No one wasted a bullet nor engaged in any hot and heavy duels with the men around the freight wagons.

Fletcher clenched his fists. This was insane. It was even worse, it was murderous. After having it all his way for so long, Buster Munzer was finally surrounded, cut off, and out-numbered. But he wasn't giving up, and that meant he'd get those men with him killed. Flint had led his people from the jailhouse up inside the livery-barn where they could fire almost at will into the backs of Buster's hench-men. While Fletcher watched a man threw up both arms, staggered out into the roadway and fell face down. Another one crumpled, sprawled across an ash wagon-tongue and rolled back and forth holding his thigh.

Fletcher eased back and stood up. He yelled loudly for the fighting to stop. He kept on yelling too, even after most of the guns had gone silent. Kept at it until the final volley was fired from over in the liverybarn. For a few moments after that there lingered only the diminishing echoes. Fletcher eased up to the corner of his building.

'Buster; it's all over for you. Flint Manly's behind you with men. I'm around here with more guns. You've lost nearly all those fools who mistakenly stood by you. Walk out from behind those wagons. If you don't the boys atop this building will pick you off one at a time. You haven't a chance in this world.'

There arose a dismal wail from that wounded man with the smashed upper leg, over where he lay wallowing in roadway dust. For almost ten seconds that was the only sound. Finally, a man's harsh, hoarse voice called back to Fletcher.

'Sheriff Markley; this here's Doc Johnson. I've had enough. There are just three of us left, not countin' Buster. We'll—'

The voice went silent. Fletcher was tempted to peek around his corner. He thought he knew what had happened to Johnson: He'd been slugged over the head. Munzer cried out, next. 'Markley; I'll bring in the army. I'll telegraph for troops. You're incitin' an insurrection. You're causin' an armed revolt against the authorities o' this county. *I'll never surrender to you; never!'*

A carbine cracked. It was the only sound for some moments. Fletcher twisted and looked upwards. That gun had been fired from atop the building. He eased back down again and pushed his head out, taking a strong risk. He had an idea that had been young Alf up there. He'd seen enough of the liveryman's kind of shooting to know that if Alf'd had Munzer in his sights when he'd fired that final shot of the battle, Munzer was down now, either dead or close to it.

No one spoke now. No one moved. The last disappearing echo from that last gunshot faded out entirely. Sunlight burnt sharply against the dissolving gunsmoke in the roadway, thickest down around those riddled freight wagons. It was so still Fletcher's ears rang from the silence. He eased out a little farther, straining to see under or around those wagons.

A man's arm came over the side of the last freight rig, waving a hat weakly. The silence ran on. Fletcher sucked back, jack-knifed up onto his feet, flinched when he forgot to favour his bad leg, then put aside his gun and stretched for a hand to support himself upon the building.

Finally, after that long and eerie wait, a voice sang out, but it didn't come from among the wagons. It came from the overhead roof. It was Alf. He said, 'Sheriff Markley; I shot Munzer. There are two men in that last wagon. I think one of 'em's hit—the feller waving his hat. There's another hurt feller down there too, shot in the hip or somethin'. I can't see Munzer any more, but when I fired he went down. He's behind the last wagon.'

Fletcher listened to all that, then stepped up and called over. 'Flint! Will! Howard! Can you fellers see any of them?'

Duran answered back. 'We can see Munzer. He's down back there behind the wagon all right, but from here it's hard to tell whether he's playin' 'possum or not.'

Flint Manly was less speculative and more practical. 'I'll find out,' he said, and Fletcher expected another gunshot, but it didn't come. No sound of any kind came for a moment, then Manly called out again. 'Fletcher? He isn't dead but if you want to talk to him you'd better hurry. That lad on the rooftop hit him hard.'

Fletcher stepped out into plain sight. Nothing happened. He started walking. Still nothing happened. From the edge of his vision he saw Broken Bow riders and armed townsmen as well, begin to filter out of dog-trots up and down the northward roadway. Some discreetly stepped back into recessed doorways here and there, but the longer this strange hush prevailed the bolder they got.

Fletcher mounted the plankwalk out front of the liverybarn, palmed his ivory-butted sixgun and side-stepped quickly around behind the wagons. There was a dead man lying half on the sidewalk, half in the dirt of the roadway. Twenty feet ahead Buster Munzer was being propped against the giant rear wheel of one of the wagons by Flint Manly and Will Duran. Howard Harrison was standing behind them, legs spread, carbine up across his body for instant use.

Fletcher stopped, holstered his weapon, gazed a moment at Munzer, then walked on, let himself down upon his good leg and looked closely when Flint opened the wounded man's riding jacket. The wound was as Flint had said—fatal.

Munzer's eyes were already beginning to cloud over. He recognised Fletcher though, and whispered a hard curse at him. Fletcher shook his head, looking up higher, into the dying man's face. 'Why, Buster?' he softly inquired. 'What in hell ever made you do all this?'

Munzer's lips worked; he tried hard forming words, but there was no sound. His head rolled and he turned loose all over, sagging down a little so that Manly and Duran had to hold him up. He was dead.

Fletcher blew out a long breath, exchanged a glance with Duran and Manly, then beckoned to Howard.

When Harrison came up he said, 'Where's Cynthia?'

'At the jailhouse. Miss Whitly's up there with her. They're looking after Cowdrey.'

Fletcher nodded, then said, 'Tell the men who were over there across the road with me, it's all over. They can come over here, if they like.'

Howard walked away. Will Duran put down his carbine and settled upon both knees. Flint Manly rummaged for makings and proceeded to work up a smoke. He offered the makings around but neither Duran nor Markley were interested.

Men came walking up, all carrying rifles or carbines or shotguns. One of the last ones to get around behind the freight wagons was Alf, the sniper who had downed Buster Munzer. He gazed at the dead man, looked around into all those unsmiling, solemn faces, and put the carbine he'd picked up somewhere during all the earlier excitement, gently against the wheel of the nearest wagon. Then he started walking away, towards the liverybarn.

Fletcher gazed after him a moment then said, 'Alf; where are you going?'

The husky youth turned back. 'Same old story,' he said quietly. 'You ride into a town, get a job—if you can —then something happens and you ride on out of it headin' for the next town.'

Fletcher shook his head. 'Stay,' he said. 'Don't be in any hurry.'

Several unarmed men came pushing between the freight rigs. These were men who'd managed to stay hidden during the entire battle. One of them turned, watching Broken Bow men hand that wounded man down the side of one of the wagons, and blanched at the sight of blood. Several other silent, tired looking men got the uninjured man out of the same wagon and pushed him over towards Fletcher Markley, after disarming him.

Finally, those unarmed men sidled in close to where Fletcher and Flint Manly were standing with Will Duran, beside the final fatality of the fight. One of them said, after noisily clearing his throat, 'Sheriff—er—Mister Markley. 'We've held an *ad hoc* meeting of the Town Council as we were walking down here an'—'

'Save it,' growled Fletcher turning to burn those men with a hard, bitter look. 'I wouldn't be your sheriff again if you tripled the pay.'

'But Fletcher,' protested one of the councilmen. 'That's just what we had in mind. That, an' of course a formal apology in public for lettin' Frank an' Buster an' those others stampede us into firing you.'

'Go hold another *ad hoc* meeting,' growled Fletcher. 'Whatever that is; then wash the taste out of your mouths up at Will's saloon.'

'But Sheriff...'

Fletcher said, 'All right, boys, I'll make it plainer. *Go—to—hell!*'

A hertofore quiet member of this perspiring group, evidently conscious that the cowmen were getting a big smile out of this, said, 'Fletcher; we've got to have law an' order. No one knows that better'n you ought to— after what's just happened. Who else can we get if you won't hire back on?'

Fletcher didn't even hesitate. He pointed over where Howard Harrison was standing. 'There's your sheriff,' he said. Then turned and pointed at Alf. 'And there's your deputy.' He dropped his arm, gazed a moment upon the councilmen, and finally his voice softened a little towards them. 'You were right. Not in being ramrodded into firing me, nor in appointing a damned crazy man to take my place. But in believing I'm too old for this line of work any more. I am. I learned that a couple of days back. This is a young man's business and I've just pointed out to you the two best young men I know of around here to take it over. But that's up to you.'

He started limping away. One of the townsmen said softly, 'Fletcher; what can you do; where are you going?'

Flint Manly, thoughtfully smoking with his eyes pinched nearly closed, said, 'It's up to Fletcher of course, but I was just thinkin'. What I need out at Broken Bow is a first-class rangeboss. After all, I'm even older'n Fletcher, an' I'd like to take it easy now.'

Fletcher halted and slowly turned. He and Flint traded a long, steady look, then Fletcher said, 'You're doin' me a favour, Flint.'

Manly uttered a mild curse and spat out his smoke. 'Not by a damned sight I'm not, Fletcher. I run a business, not a charity outfit. I've wanted to mention this to you for a year, but it just never seemed like you'd be interested. It pays a sight more'n you got aroun' here riskin' your hide for a bunch of ingrates, an' if you like, you can even live here in town.'

Fletcher looked quizzical. 'I'll take the job,' he said. 'Only, why would I want to live here in town?'

Flint pointed behind Fletcher and got red in the face. Fletcher turned. Angela Whitly was standing back there smiling up at him. Beside her was Cynthia Whitson. Cynthia was smiling at young Howard Harrison.

Will Duran cleared his throat and glowered at the grinning men. 'Well,' he said briskly, 'let's clean up around here. This doggoned town is a disgrace. 'Come on, men; lend a hand. If it's all completed by high noon I'll stand the first two rounds up at my saloon.'

Everyone jerked to life and began moving, even the somewhat disgraced Town Councilmen.

ov - 11/02

B